Hanged for l'Acadie

a Kesk8a story

www.crowecreations.ca

Hanged for l'Acadie

First Crowe Creations Print Publication July 2021.

This is a work of fiction set against a backdrop of history. Except for actual historical persons, almost all characters are fictional so any resemblance to persons living or dead is a coincidence. And even the opinions about actual historical persons are those of fictional characters, not this author's. This author's actual ancestors, Claude Guidry and Marguerite Petitpas, and their son, J-B, et al. in this book, were real. Kesk8a was real, too.

Front cover photo © iStock, photo ID:493938588
Cover Design © 2021 Crowe Creations
Interior design by Crowe Creations
Text set in Garamond; headings in Clarity Gothic SF

Crowe Creations
ISBN: 978-1-927058-81-7

Dedicated to The Children

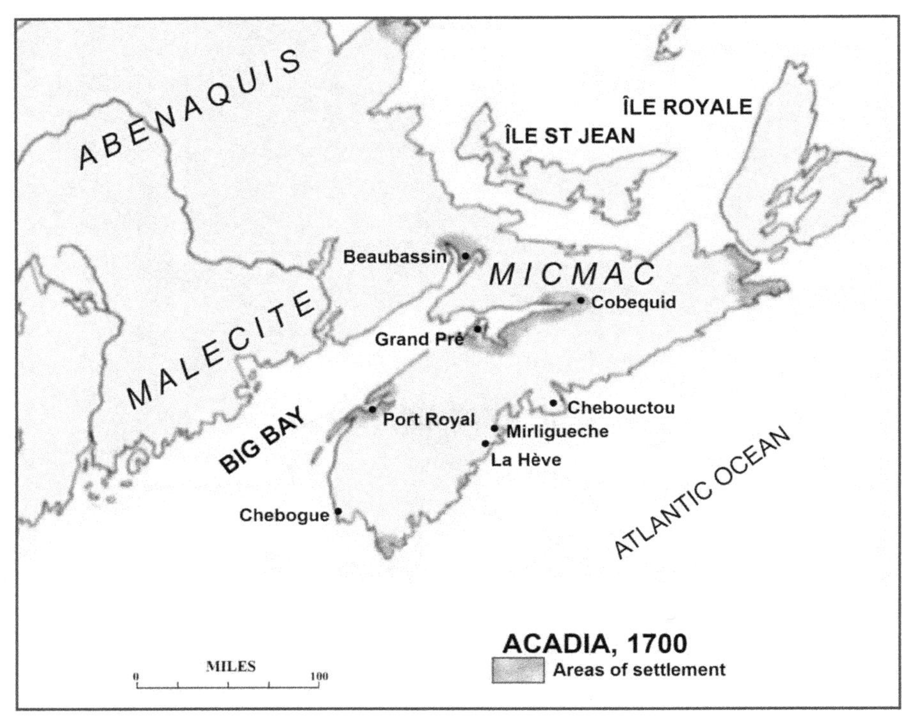

NOTE: "Settlement" is settlement by the Newcomers.

Foreword

When I first decided to write about what happened to my Acadian cousins, it was supposed to be one book. [Insert laughter.] There will be six, as long as the crik don't rise, that is. As I did my research on the Acadian people, I learned more and more about myself, about where I had come from [spiritually] on my father's side, my family and my millions of Cajun cousins. Then more about humanity—or, as you will see in some cases, the lack thereof.

This book, Book 4 in the Kesk8a series, was exceptionally difficult to write because I couldn't wing it with imaginary characters that I like to use so I can show what went on in the historical background without getting into trouble for saying something "that didn't happen to him or her." Some of the characters in this book were realer than real: my ancestor Claude Guédry's second son, Jean-Baptiste Guédry; Jean-Baptiste's son Jean-Baptiste Guédry le Jeune; Jean-Baptiste's two brothers-in-law, James and Philippe Mius; John Missel; and the "three Indians" who were presumed drowned. Oh, and "an Indian woman and two children" that history says, "nothing is known about the fate of"; and Jean-Baptiste's wife, Madeleine Marguerite Moise Morning Star. Claude's ninth child with Marguerite Petitpas was Pierre Guédry dit LaBine. Pierre is my 6th great grandfather so I now know on whose DNA I can blame my stubbornness.

What made it so extra difficult was that anywhere we look online about "the hanging of two Acadians and three Indians" we'll find the story about J-B and the others who were involved in this tragedy. It's all there. I even found the transcript of the trial. (*See*, Appendix.) I was, essentially, forced to "keep to the script" while writing the ending of this book.

Another thing that made writing this difficult was the current events that blew up all over the media (and about time, too!) while I was approximately mid-way through it. Keep in mind that I decided on this particular book's subject matter long before I published Book 1 of the series in 2015. This book is not about current events, this book is about events that were happening in the 17th and 18th centuries. But they are obviously still going on! How hard did I cry when I heard about those little children's bodies being found? Having already written three and half books in this series made it feel like I knew each and every single one of them. Family. Finally home. Tears of sorrow but tears of relief.

SW
2021

"The only thing that can predict the future is the past."—Keskoua

One

1726

I can still hear Marguerite's voice and I think I always will: "Merci à Dieu que Claude est mort. If he were not already dead, this would surely have killed him."

I tried to comfort her by placing my hand on her shoulder but she pushed me away as though I were a go´gwejij, a spider.

"I can't believe they did that. Is there any word beyond maudit for the Maudits anglaises? Puissent-ils tous pourrir en Enfer."

"I don't think even Hell would want the likes of those people," I said, trying to comfort her in another way.

"Now is not the time to be using humor, Keskoua. Poor Morning Star. She has lost not only a son, perhaps two, but a husband, two brothers, perhaps three, and a dear family friend to those bâtards and their concept of what is right and what is wrong. And other friends are missing."

Again, I tried to comfort her, without success.

"And I? I have lost one son and probably two grandsons. A son and a grandson hanged! Could there be any more humiliating or disgraceful death? And for piracy of all things. The furthest thing from who J-B is—was!—that could ever be. And his son. Fourteen years old and dead. Hanged. Hanged! Barely fourteen. By days, fourteen, for the love of Christ! Mon Dieu. I am finally happy that Claude is dead."

But I'm getting ahead of myself, aren't I?

Two

Everything had changed. Everything. I was no longer sixty-one winters old. I was now sixty-one *years* old. And if I said anything different—especially if I said it in Mi´gmaq—I would hear about it. Everything was in English now, not just the language, but inside our heads. We were expected to live by the rules of a book that none of us had read. At least, not my people. And when I asked Marguerite one day, if she had read this book, she recoiled from me with her eyes wide and filled with fear.

"Jamais! Never! It is on the Index Librorum Prohibitorum."

"The what?"

"The list of books forbidden by the Catholic Church."

I couldn't help myself. I grasped my stomach and leaned over laughing. "You're supposed to go by the rules of a book you're not allowed to read?" Even with Marguerite chastising me, I continued to laugh.

"There's nothing funny, Keskoua. That book is on the list for a reason. And here the English are trying to force us to read it. To adhere to its precepts. Well, it's more the New Englanders who are that strict. And not all of them. Réellement, actually, it's only one group and that group is fearful of everything. We are all aware of that!"

"Oh. That felt good," I said. "To its what? Its pre…?"

"Precepts. Rules to live by."

"We don't go by rules. You know that."

Now it was Marguerite's turn to laugh. "You don't go by rules. All the old ladies in the village—"

"Please. We're called the Grandmothers."

"See?"

"Oh, stop."

"No. I won't stop. All the old ladies in the village watch every move that everyone makes and they talk about it and complain if anyone steps outside their perceived notion of what is right and what is not right and if anyone crosses those barriers, they are tossed out of the village to fend for themselves—"

"It's called being banished," I said. "And I got banished for two days once."

"I'm not surprised." Marguerite glared at me from under her eyebrows. "… and perhaps even starve to death in the process. Don't give me any of that nonsense about no rules for your people." She shook her head. "No. No. I'm sorry. I don't like saying yours and mine and us and them and we and they and I and you when it comes to my extended family here. *Our* people. We are all 'our people' here. Except for them. Right?"

I laughed, hugged her, then stepped back. I knew what the answer would be but I asked her anyway. "So, did you read it?"

"I told you. It's forbidden." Here, she turned her face away from me.

"You *did*, didn't you? And don't lie. That's a sin, isn't it? Does it say it in that book that it's a sin to lie?"

"I think I left something on the stove." She turned fully away from me now, her skirts billowing as she headed toward the path that led to her house.

I called after her. "Do you have to go to Confession now?"

"What?" She stopped.

I caught up with her. "Or is it na to´q, is it all right, to lie to your friends?"

"Everything is na to´q. And everything is not na to´q. It all depends on the circumstances. Sometimes it's permitted to even kill someone and other times it isn't."

I wasn't finding anything funny anymore and I think Marguerite read this on my face. I was much better than I used to be at hiding what I was thinking, but I wasn't perfect.

"It depends on whether that someone believes the same things you do. Or not. If they don't believe in the same things you do, you may kill them. If they do believe in the same things you do, you may not kill them."

I would never understand the English. "What about lies, though? What does it say about lies?" I was thinking about all those flames licking at my legs and burning my clothes off if I ended up in Hell like I had been hearing about from the Fathers—the priests—since I was young. I lied to the English all the time. Even when I didn't have to. It was fun.

"About lies it says, You must not bear false witness against your neighbor."

"So… that means you *can* bear false witness against people who *aren't* your neighbor?"

It was good to hear and see Marguerite laugh. It was good to see anybody laugh these days. Like I said, everything was different. But, to survive, we would all have to adapt. Or at least appear to adapt if we wanted to stay alive.

But here I am, getting ahead of myself again. Let's go back to when Mak and I decided to move to Mirligueche. Yes, we were going to move from the area of Port Royal—sorry, Annapolis Royal now—to the east.

Three

August, 1726

Mak's inn had been doing so very well over the years at Annapolis Royal, he started one in Chebogue. When that one began doing well, he decided—*we* decided—to start a third one in Mirligueche. And to move there. Many of our friends were there now. Some of them traveled back and forth between Mirligueche and the Annapolis Royal area on a regular basis. Claude and Marguerite, and their children and grandchildren, had been doing so for years.

Mak and I were not the only ones building inns near various ports along the coast. With the great influx of people from south of us, from England and especially from Scotland (this was Nova Scotia, "New Scotland," after all) there was a demand for inns. Not everyone wanted to *live* in Nova Scotia, though. Many were merely passing through, or delivering or collecting goods, or taking note of how they could make a fortune from our resources. They began to call our inn, and the other inns, "public houses." Pubs, for short.

At first, because these pubs, because of their purpose, were built close to forts full of soldiers and to ports where so many strangers came and went, we all thought there would be problems having so many establishments where men could get beer, wine, and what they called spirits. I thought that was an interesting word for alcohol. "Spirits." As a healer, I had helped many people through the torment of withdrawal from drinking alcohol in its many forms. Those recovering would see a lot more than spirits most of the time, so perhaps the word "spirits" was a good one, if only to serve as an ignored warning, an I-told-you-so. As it turned out, the one good thing about the English was that they seemed to behave themselves in the public section of the inns where the drinking went on. Did I say "generally speaking"? If not, that's what I meant to say: "Generally speaking, the English behaved themselves in the pubs."

We hadn't given a name to our inn at Annapolis Royal. Not because we didn't have any idea what to name it, but because *any* idea we had, probably would have caused problems.

One of these problems was that the English liked to collect taxes and they liked to have rules. Setting up inns here and there where people could eat and drink, and pubs where local people could perhaps congregate to plan overthrows, did not suit the English intent of controlling everybody and every little thing. If any one of us had even hinted at actually running a business—making money—rather than merely having friends over for a visit and a pint, the tax collector would have been knocking at our door. And so would the English authorities. But the English authorities would tend to be in the persons of the actual soldiers who frequented these establishments in the first place. I've said it before and I swear I'll be saying it on my deathbed: I'll never understand these people.

Another problem was having Mak be the owner of an inn, let alone the host of a room open to the public, a pub. Because of his dark skin, some of the New Englanders could not accept his authority as innkeeper to start with. To be running a pub was unthinkable. In their minds, a slave was a slave, even a free one. "If God did not want you to be a slave, He would not have made you be born a Negro."

We "savages" were looked at from the top of people's noses, too.

And the Acadians? The Acadians were Catholics. What could be worse in the minds of the New England Puritans than a Catholic? Oh, except that most of the Acadians and most of the "savages" were now mixed together. So much so that even we couldn't tell each other apart even if we'd wanted to. Even the mention of mixed race around some of the Puritan women made them fan their faces faster with the horror of the thought. Did not their Sixth Commandment expressly forbid adulterating the white race? There would come a time when "mixed" people would learn what the meaning of that word, horror, meant. But look at me. Here I am getting ahead of myself again.

Two of the New England Raiders we had met when some of us had gone to Grand Pré when Benny was burning everything down, had become good friends with Mak and me. Zeke was working at Mak's inn. Abraham, who called himself Hammy, so everybody else did, too, had become the local pigeon messenger caretaker.

Hammy was also good at carving things so, to hang over the entrance to our inn, he had carved a wooden pigeon in flight with a birch bark message tied around its leg. It was an actual strip of birch bark that we had to change every now and again because the weather would wear it out. Nosy fingers wore it out, too. It was constantly being removed, read, and replaced. Nothing other than the word "Welcome" was ever written on this strip of birch bark but we had made a lot of suggestions among ourselves that we didn't dare try, but had good laughs about.

This sign was disliked—feared?—by certain New Englanders, I think even more than the thoughts of Mak owning something. Something he had built with his own hands and had hired people to help build, or had had people helping him build for nothing. Something he made money from. Their money. Nothing made Mak smile more than to hold out his hand and have these hating New Englanders deposit coins into the palm of it.

Hammy had taken this pigeon messenger sign idea from a family of snipes that had moved in behind our inn close to where he kept his pigeons. A snipe will do many things to lead a predator away from its nest. It will even fake injury and put its own self in danger. This pigeon sign, for many of the New Englanders then, not just the hating ones, depicted the inn as a place for spies to congregate.

"If they're looking for spies," Hammy had explained. "They might not notice that a man from Africa is making a good deal of money selling them food and drink while they're staring at everyone else."

We had a lot of fun with all of this, too, of course. Most of the new people accepted Mak as the proprietor of Pigeon Message Inn—their name, not ours—but as I said, there were some who didn't.

When these new people would debark from one of the ships at the port, and would enter the inn to see Mak behind the bar or giving instructions to our chef, or to the servers, they would be shocked at seeing a dark-skinned man in charge. We soon got to recognize these people and what their attitude would be by the way they treated those who worked on the docks, so Zeke would pretend *he* was the owner of the inn. Mak would then curl over to be able to look up at Zeke and Mak would say things like, "You know I can't read nor write, massah. So I have no idea what's in those pigeon messages. Massah Hammy will know. Ask Massah Hammy." And he would scurry off into the kitchen area leaving us to try to keep the laughter from bursting out of ourselves. It was both funny and sad. And yes, anger inducing at the same time, but it helped us deal with these people. Most of them ended up accepting Mak as proprietor and owner of Pigeon Message Inn. Eventually. Most of them. Not all.

It wasn't "these people," really. If you looked at it another way, they were perhaps of better character than those who *didn't* hate. "These people" followed their Book's instructions whether they believed in those instructions or not because they thought it was the right thing to do. Not merely that they would go to Hell if they didn't. That took strength. Or was it strength? This got me thinking about what Marguerite had said about the Grandmothers. How the Grandmothers talked among themselves and decided who was good and who was bad. That they decided who and why any one of us would be banished. And for how long. That the Grandmothers controlled us without even having a book to point to. Were our Grandmothers—not all, only the ones who always did this—any better than those Puritans who always did *that*?

Most New Englanders fit in with the "Catholics," the "savages" and the "Negros" as though we were all family, like we Mi´gmaq and Acadians and dark-skinned people did with each other and with those who accepted us. As I said, not all were warm and loving. All sides had those whose opinions and experiences pushed or pulled their thinking like the tide near Minas Basin pushed or pulled everything in its grasp: irresistible, unrelenting, too strong not to succumb to.

One New England family, a family of Puritans, a family that fit in with all of us and all of them, made the most exquisite furniture. Hammy worked with them, too. He worked hard with his pigeons, but this did not take up his entire days and nights. He could do both so he did. Being in the middle like that, and getting and sending pigeons from all sides and all points of view, made Hammy an important person in our community. So everyone was nice to him. Some even suggested he should start putting out a newspaper like they had done in Boston, since all the news came to him. This made Hammy laugh, "Perhaps I shall put out a newspaper then. It will contain only what I am allowed to make public. Therefore, it will be invisible. Therefore, how do you know I am not already 'putting out a newspaper'?"

Mak had hired this family—father, mother, two sons and one daughter—to make the bureaus and beds for the rooms in the inn at Chebogue, and the tables and chairs for the public room. Hammy had been instrumental in helping with the setting-up of our Pigeon Messenger Inn so was invaluable to this family with his advice. They had just completed similar pieces for our new inn at Mirligueche. They had even constructed a huge bar for one end of the main public room.

And this was why we were all standing on the dock at Annapolis Royal, holding our collective breath while sailors and other workers loaded these precious items onto a ship bound for Mirligueche. Mak and I would be boarding the ship that had just slid in against the dock behind it. Mak would not be going anywhere until everything had been loaded. Loaded to Mak's satisfaction. I could understand this. I was similarly obsessed with my munti's contents, my healing bag.

Mak leaned his head close to mine as he said, "What did she say then? J-B has heard nothing?"

"As far as she knows—as far as anybody knows—they haven't released them yet."

"It's been ages since they signed that thing."

"Two months and yes, it does feel like forever. I can't imagine what it must be like to not know where your child is. What they're doing to him. To wonder if he's in prison or if they sold him as…" I whispered this part: "… a slave."

"More likely sold, I've heard. I can't believe any human being can treat another as a possession or toy or machine solely because of the color of their skin."

"And they're dangling it like bait in front of J-B, trying to make him do things that aren't in his nature."

"Young Paul would be what…? Eleven years old now?"

"Uh. Yes. He would be by now. He was taken when he was eight. So yes. Eleven. J-B's trying to stay neutral and they're… They're pressuring him."

Mak shook his head and put an arm around behind my shoulders so he could pull me closer. "I can't imagine. I cannot imagine. I know I'd crack. I'm sure I'd be out killing people by now."

"They'd just kill you back and you can't do anything if you're dead, can you?"

"Probably not."

"*Probably* not?" Mak always lifted my spirits no matter what serious events we were discussing. "Marguerite told me he has something in mind though. But she's terrified that he might actually try to do it."

"Oh? Are you allowed to share— Hey!" Mak removed his arm from my shoulders to wave at the men loading our furniture. "Slow down with that. Don't bang it on anything."

Shouts from both the dock and the ship's deck followed and the quick forward motion of the net holding a large open-front armoire up in the air stopped. The net swung back and forth making the armoire glint in the sunlight. Its high gleam was from the beeswax coating it. Hours and hours of work by those who'd built it. Mak didn't want it scratched. I didn't either. Matching the color of the beeswax would mean sending the armoire back to where it came from to be repaired. And that could take a year. The color depended on the flowers the bees visited. Mak had told me that. And he'd said that's why he wanted the armoire done in Montréal. He'd seen examples of what they produced there. The English weren't pleased that he had supported the business of a "bloody Frenchman."

A voice called out: "Sorry, Mak." This was followed by what I imagined would be curse words going back and forth between two men, but in a language I did not know.

Mak put his arm back around me. "Where were we?"

"She says someone is trying to influence J-B to—"

This time, Mak released me to stride toward the loading dock. "This is a valuable piece of furniture. Go easy with it. There isn't another like it anywhere."

I heard Marguerite's voice: "You tell them, Mak. They're not listening to me. Damn fools."

Marguerite and her son Pierre and her daughter Franny were leaning over the rail of the ship, watching the men load the furniture. Pierre was nearly thirty years old now. Time goes by so quickly. I remember when he was born. Her daughter would be twenty-three. Marguerite had come to visit friends, so she said, and was heading back to Mirligueche. She was now almost sixty-five winters old—sorry, *years*—and not in the best of health, so that was why Pierre and Franny had come with her. So she said. I suspected there were other reasons she had come because this time, they had brought huge suitcases that were now almost bursting with supplies. Marguerite had refused to tell me what those supplies were, but I suspected it was food. Mak and I would be hunting for, fishing for and purchasing our own personal supplies when we got to our new inn. And we would hire others for getting what we would need for feeding our patrons. I didn't have to wonder why they had come all this way to purchase these things. J-B was not the only son of Claude and Marguerite who was being pressured to take sides between the English who now controlled Nova Scotia and the French who still controlled Île Royale. Pierre was too.

But this thought skipped through my mind like a kingfisher had flown over the top of my head and scooped it out.

Marguerite was in the process of promising Mak, me, Zeke, Hammy, the furniture maker and every member of his family and even our regular pub patrons, that, "Yes, I will be certain that everything arrives and gets taken off safely. J-B will see to it, too. He will ensure that everything ends up in the exact, right, correct, specific, explicit place in your new—" And this was where she was interrupted by a burst of excitement behind us.

We all looked.

Children were pointing to the sky and crying out. "Look! Look at all the pigeons!"

Perhaps fifteen or twenty birds were flying in. Fast. They were disappearing behind the inn. Where Hammy's pigeon station was.

"That many messages all at once? What's going on?" Mak returned to my side. "I didn't think you were that important anymore."

He laughed. I didn't.

"You know. Since you… Since you 'retired' from being the one everybody—and I swear everybody—reaches out to for, I swear, any little thing."

"What's going on?" called Marguerite from the ship's rail. "Is it someone's birthday? What day is today? Did I miss something?" She laughed as she threw her arms around her children. "It's a bon voyage celebration for us, mes enfants. Imagine that."

Her son tried to pull away from her grasp without success.

"Look, everyone." Marguerite continued laughing. "We're famous."

Marguerite's daughter leaned forward to see past Marguerite at her brother. Even from where I stood on the dock, I could feel the concern coming out of her as Pierre pulled a scarf up to cover his lower face. I made note of it. Franny whispered something to Marguerite.

Mouth agape now, and no longer smiling, Marguerite released Pierre who disappeared from the ship's rail.

"This could be something serious, Mak. And I'm no more or less important than anybody else around here."

"Not to me." He put his arm across my shoulders again and squeezed me closer to him. "You are my everything."

I tried to roll my eyes in pretended anger but that never works when you're trying not to smile at the same time. Or when you're worried at the same time about a friend's son. Or a friend's sons. A friend's grandson.

"Well?" demanded Marguerite. "What's going on?"

"Is she always this… this intense?" asked the furniture maker's wife.

"She's been having cauchemars," I replied.

"Coosh what?"

"Cauchemars. It's French. Means nightmares."

"Ah."

"About J-B."

"Ah yes. I know about his missing son. Everybody does. Terrible."

"She says something bad is going to happen to J-B. She's been having the dreams for years. And it looks like—" I pushed my lips together. I dared not say anything further about what was going on with her other son, Pierre. It must have gotten worse for him to risk coming all the way to Annapolis Royal, of all places, for supplies.

My thoughts were interrupted by the concerned furniture maker's wife.

"Oh. I think I'd be intense, too, then." She hung her head. "I'm going to have to stop judging you people."

"I'll go ask Hammy what's going on." But as I turned, he was running toward us.

"Keskoua! A message. For you."

"See?" said Mak.

"It's from Chief Jumping Robin's village. From Agada, I think. It's got pink coloring on it."

It felt like everyone on both the ships and the dock was watching me as I began to carefully peel the message open.

"The other pigeons have nothing on them. Nothing. Something's wrong. And they all came back. All of them. All of the ones from Chief Jumping Robin's village."

The message was open in my fingers.

Hammy continued his worried talking as though I could do anything about the situation. "They have no pigeons there anymore. What if there's an emergency?"

I read Agada's message:

Need help.

"Send her a message!" I told Hammy. "Tell her I'm on my way!"

Hammy ran back toward the inn.

I kissed Mak and told him, "I have to go. I'm needed."

"Do you want me to wait?"

I stared at him.

He kissed me. "May the wind and the tides bring you safely into my arms again. I'll see you in Mirligueche, *mpenzi*, my love."

Four

Every so often, Hammy would have collected enough messenger pigeons to warrant a boat trip here and there to exchange pigeons at various villages and settlements. When it was time to go to Flower Stalk's village, or to Chief Matuwes's village which was further up the coast from Flower Stalk's, I usually went with him. Flower Stalk was a good friend, as was Agada. Because Agada was the healer at Chief Matuwes's village, when we took our pigeons there and collected theirs, I could spend time visiting with her, exchanging not only news. Sometimes sicknesses or injuries came along that were difficult to treat, or different entirely from what we were used to, so it was always best to have someone to discuss ideas with and learn new ones from, even though, as Mak would say, I was now a "retired" healer.

My daughter Su´n had been at my side since her birth so knew everything I knew. My sons had been at my side, too, but neither of them had taken an interest in becoming either a healer or a storyteller. They had families now and were thinking of moving away from the village. What was left of our village. Most of our young men had gone away soon after their Spirit Quests. There wasn't much for them to do anymore. Their trapping and hunting and fishing areas had been taken over by those they had started calling the "Invaders." Our young women had followed them. Some of these young people were never seen or heard from again. We had ideas, but no one would speak that word aloud.

Su´n had already taken over almost all my duties. My brother's woman, Wasueg, excelled at midwifery so she mostly looked after the women who were going to be having babies. Like I had done for many years, Su´n was also learning from the surgeons at the fort. The French surgeons had enjoyed helping me and now, to my relief, the English surgeons were glad to help her with new medical information, even instruments, coming from England and Europe. They sought and appreciated and used her advice, too, like they had mine. However, these latest surgeons would never *admit* to using our advice because, like me, she was not only a "savage" but female. Or should I say that as, "not only female but a 'savage'?" I don't know which one they thought was worse.

Agada and Su´n had become friends, so that made me feel better about moving to Mirligueche. As I had done, Su´n would be able to reach out to Agada when needed and the other way around.

Geneviève, who had sometimes taken over my duties as healer when I was away, had not been seen by anyone for nearly three years now. She had often disappeared into the bush with her bad memories, but because of her advanced age, we all thought, perhaps, she had finally gone on her Journey and would not return. Rabbit Woman, who always stepped in when I was away, and always helped me when I got busy, and who was now doing the same thing for Su´n, was also elderly and not doing well at all. Su´n would have to stay in the village to tend to Rabbit Woman and to anyone else who needed her. Her own daughter, my first grandchild, who was training to be a healer and doing well at it, was not yet ready—or should I say not yet willing?—to be left alone, even with Wasueg there to help her if needed.

Hammy and I had a lot to do and a short time to do it in before we had to leave, on foot, across the land, to get to the Big Bay before the tide changed. We not only had to replenish the supply of our messenger pigeons at what was now Chief Jumping Robin's village, but Agada needed me. I knew it would be for something serious this time. She usually said more in her messages. I was worried. Chief Jumping Robin was new to the village and to us. I had yet to meet him, and pigeon messages from Agada and Flower Stalk held little to nothing about him. I hadn't gone with Hammy since Snow Blinding Month, February, when I went to be with Matuwes during her final days.

Did Agada's urgent message have something to do with the released messenger pigeons? The only means of communication at a distance they had other than by foot over land to reach out for help? Had something happened? A tidal wave? A raid? An attack? A fire? An explosion of some sort? Or was she having problems with her daughter? Sofia was now fifteen years old. A young woman. Young women of that age often went through difficult times trying to understand what life was all about, and how they would—or would not—fit into it. And Agada was alone. Second Son—Secky—Sofia's father, had gone on his Journey when she was four years old and Agada had been alone ever since. Is this why Agada needed me? Because she was alone and had no one to confide in? Did others need me, too?

I would soon find out.

Five

Hammy and I didn't ever go by ship from the harbor at Annapolis Royal when we went to our friends' villages up the coast of the Big Bay, even though it might be somewhat safer. There were no ports for vessels that size where we wanted to go. We would have had to pay money in the first place, then pay extra money to have the ship drop anchor wherever the captain wished to drop it so he could wait safely while someone put us into a small boat and rowed us to shore. And that depended on weather, too. Once on shore, we would have had to hack our way through probably unfamiliar bush to get to where we wanted to be. If we could even find it from there.

No. We always walked overland to the Big Bay where there were boats and large canoes and people calling themselves "captain just for the hell of it." These were mostly experienced fishers and ferriers, both men and women.

But there were also young men (mostly New Englanders) looking for ways to make quick money for themselves and their families, too. These would offer their services, and their tiny rowboats, to take people all the way into Minas Basin. *Into* Minas Basin, they would say. They would also state their fees for doing so and these were usually high. These announcements would give fair warning to any potential passenger that these were amateurs and not to be trusted.

Experienced captains would offer to take people *toward* Minas Basin, or *almost to* Minas Basin's mouth. I say this because nobody in a rowboat, using the tide for traveling, would even *think* about taking their passengers any further than *almost* to the mouth of Minas Basin. And these young men had only rowboats to offer. We had to rely entirely on tide and wind and the experience of the captains to get there within a reasonable time.

The experienced, with their barges or large boats and canoes—all with sails of some sort—would transport us up or down the coast in exchange for food or whatever we had to offer that they might need or want. If we had nothing they needed or wanted, they would still take us. That was their way which was our way and nobody owed anybody anything. Ever. And no one had ever been injured or lost on these trips up and down the coast. Not that I knew of at least.

It was no longer required to have several people, usually village children, help get the messenger pigeons in their cages to the area of the boats. Hammy had designed a special travois that could hold up to twenty cages when the extension was added. The cages were made of cedar so weighed next to nothing. Two people could carry the travois on their shoulders or, without the extension, one person could drag it when there were only a few cages on it. It had detachable wheels that could withstand bumps against rocks and snagging tree roots.

We were bringing more than usual with us this time, so had to use the extender section, and it would take two of us to carry it. Two birds to a cage so a bird a day for a moon, twenty-eight days. And one extra for sending out on arrival to let those back home know we'd arrived safely. There was room for three or even four in a cage, but Hammy didn't like to crowd them. He said it was because they didn't like it. I had never thought that about pigeons. I had no idea how Hammy could know what pigeons liked or didn't like, they were always so quiet and peaceful and serene and seemed to accept whatever Hammy did to them. They had never even made eye contact with me. Was that because they felt no respect coming from me? I wasn't sure if not liking to be crowded would cause the pigeons to strike one another with a wing or grab a beak with a claw. I decided I would start to pay attention to them. I would watch to see how they handled disputes between and among themselves, especially the one cage that would contain the extra pigeon.

To help transport the pigeons over land this time, a young man I had never met insisted on coming along with Hammy and me. I could tell by his complexion and facial structure that he was not one of our people, he was perhaps Acadian. Maybe even French, English or Dutch. But his hair and the band around his head, his clothing—especially his moccasins and leg wrappings—his jacket and his manner and his accent told me otherwise. Was he mixed? Since I had never laid eyes on him, I assumed he had arrived on the ship that Marguerite and her children had just left port on, although I hadn't seen him debark from it. Perhaps he'd arrived on the ship my Mak was about to leave on.

"I suppose I'll just supervise then," I said. "Let me know if you need anything." I raised my nose in the air, pretending to act like the ones I'd seen bossing people around near the fort and especially at Mirligueche the times I'd been there.

The young man laughed.

Hammy smiled at the young man and told him, "That's not really any different from usual for her."

The young man's eyebrows squeezed together. "Oh?"

Hammy laughed. "It's quite all right, she can't help it. Ask anyone."

The young man looked at me then and asked, "Is he telling a joke?"

I glared at Hammy. "I certainly hope so."

Hammy laughed. "I like to tease her. Ready?"

"Yes."

They hoisted the travois onto their shoulders, settled it, and began walking. Some of the pigeons had adjusted their wings on being lifted up in anticipation of having to take flight. Hammy was right. If the cage had been crowded, the pigeons would have been poking each other in the eye with the tips of their feathers.

I followed.

I heard Hammy ask the question that was hiding behind my own lips. "So, young sir, what brings you here? Or is it any of our business to ask?" Hammy knew me well.

The young man was looking for someone, he said, and had been told he could find her at Chief Jumping Robin's village.

When I asked him where he was coming from, he replied, "I came from Île Royale."

"Really. On a French ship from Louisbourg. How did you manage to do that without being detained immediately?"

"How indeed?"

"And if you could have managed that, what ship goes from Louisbourg to here anymore without being sunk along the way? Or at least held for questioning?"

"What ship indeed?"

It looked like I wouldn't be getting any more information about him or how he'd gotten here, but when I asked his name, he was open about that. His name was Bobby. And when I made a guess that he would be about seventeen years old, he confirmed it.

"Good guess," he said. "Most people assume I am much older."

Or much younger? I thought.

I asked him where the name Bobby had come from. The Grandfathers had given him the name Young Bobcat Man after his Spirit Quest, he told me. He was proud of his new name, but he went by Bobby to keep the English happy. "It's always best to keep the English happy. Is it not?"

Of course I agreed with him, but didn't say it out loud. There was something about him.

Bobby didn't seem to me to be the kind of young man who talked a lot, so I think he was talking on and on to make sure nobody asked any more questions. For the rest of the overland section of our trip, he told us how proud he was to be a man now, how he wanted to do everything and anything possible for our people like our men always did—or tried to these days—and to maintain the ways of The People no matter what.

I knew all too well how dangerous that kind of thinking could be for our young men lately. Again, I said nothing but I made a mental note: there's a lot more to him than he appears to be.

***

There were three other passengers besides Hammy, Bobby and me on the boat heading toward the village of my friend Agada. There were two elderly Acadians—one man, one woman—and a middle-aged New Englander, no doubt a Puritan because he wouldn't tell us his name. I didn't insist on getting his name from him as I was sadly aware of what New Englanders, especially Puritan New Englanders, named their children. Names like Damnation. I'd met a man with that name, but he'd called himself Nation. Hammy knew him, too. And so did our mutual friend, Zeke. I'd met them all during the attack on Grand Pré back in the summer of 1704. The elderly Acadians didn't share their names either and I knew it was because they didn't want the Puritan to point at them and start ranting at them for being devils with their French names. I didn't share my name for a similar reason. Our captain didn't offer his name either, but Bobby did. Why not? He had nothing to hide. Except his traditional clothing and his long hair and accent? After all, his *name* was English, wasn't it? And he spoke it. And well.

As the tide moved us along toward our destination, Bobby suggested, with what I imagined a Puritan might call a "devilish" look on his face, that everyone might like to play a game. I decided in my own head that this was most likely to break the uncomfortable silence that hung over us like the smell of a decaying apugjilu, a decaying skunk. One that had been badly frightened just before death. But I was wrong. One must never decide what someone else is thinking, not even after asking them to tell the truth. The game was to spot a specific animal or bird or tree or plant. The one who got the most the fastest would be the one who chose the next animal or plant to be searched for.

"I'll go first," said Bobby. "Find the squirrels."

After several minutes, our captain called out, "There's one. On the fallen pine there."

I followed his extended finger to see a tail flick behind a log. "Ah. Yes. I saw its tail."

"Anyone else?" asked Bobby after we had traveled for quite some time. "Are we still playing?"

"I recall playing this game as a child," said the elderly Acadian man. "It went a lot faster than this, I'll tell you. Perhaps it's my eyes but I haven't seen a bird since we left. Except for these." He pointed his thumb at the stack of bird cages. "And that was the only squirrel."

"So it's not just me?" I could tell that Bobby actually wanted an answer to that question. "Mostly everything everywhere in Acadia has disappeared, hasn't it?"

The nameless man spoke. "Nothing's going to be living on those bloody high rock cliffs, you silly fool."

At this, I glanced over at the pigeons who all seemed to be looking at the man with—if they'd had them—one eyebrow raised.

"It's not all rock cliffs," said the elderly Acadian man. "Look ahead there. A low area. With trees."

"But no wildlife, I'd bet," said Bobby, arms crossed, chin held high.

"What's with that negative attitude of yours, boy?" asked the nameless man. "It seems all of you people are always complaining about something or other."

There it was, the dreaded phrase, "you people." And spoken as though the nameless man hadn't noticed the absence of Mi´gmaw features on Bobby, only his attire. Were we that invisible to them?

As we neared the low area, I saw that there was a cleared-out section full of grazing cows and a few sparse trees lined up along the shore. "Where did they come from?" I asked. "They weren't there the last time I came by. Were they maybe kept indoors because of the snow? That's the last time I was through here. Hammy? You travel through here every moon— Uh. Every month. Where did they come from?"

"Are there cows on that list for your stupid game, boy? I count… twenty-five. I win."

The elderly Acadian woman spoke up. "I don't understand why they need so many cows. There are only two windows on the top floor. Two sleeping rooms then. That would indicate their family is small. Would it not?"

"I understand," said Hammy. "All too well. It was the same in New England where I come from. It's purely business. And no. All those cows weren't there the last time I came by, but the trees were already gone and the stumps uprooted. Everything was ready for them. I'm surprised the grass has grown enough to feed those cows in such a short time. But since everything here is also all about money and making money now, I suppose they can just purchase the sod and have it shipped in from somewhere."

"It's that easy?" I asked.

Bobby spoke. "It's all about money. Think of fish. We catch a few for ourselves to eat or to share with neighbors. What *they* do…" and he said the word "they" with the same disdain as the nameless man had put into his "you people" words, and he glanced at the man when he said it… "is catch as many as they can and sell them for a pence a fish."

"Now there's a thought," said the elderly Acadian man. "Then these buyers sell the fish for *two* pence each. Am I on the correct thinking path?"

"Depends on where they sell them. And to whom," answered Bobby. "If they sell them to the inns, for example, the inns will pay as low a price as they can."

"That's true," I said. "We often purchase our fish now. We need more than we can catch ourselves. And we often don't have the time to fish in the first place. If we pay too high an amount for a product, we have to increase the price for our patrons. They are not as eager to purchase what we have to offer. So we lose."

Bobby continued. "Let's say, yes, two pence each. But these, the inns will cut into pieces. Heads and tails for soup. Five bowls at even three pennies each—and it's more like a shilling a bowl—will bring in a lot. Then the rest of the fish will be cut into two pieces at perhaps a shilling or more? Lucrative, yes? One fish that cost two pence brings in much more."

"That's true," I said, now feeling somewhat guilty.

"Smart," said the elderly Acadian woman. "No wonder they are always fighting over fishing rights."

"Think about it," said Bobby. "The Invaders are taking advantage of everything."

"Invaders? Who are you calling invaders?"

"You people," said Bobby. "You people are not hunting and fishing to eat or feed your families and your neighbors. You people do it solely to make money. Just like Hammy said. That's all. Will you people go back to England once you become rich? I think some will. When everything here is gone, you'll leave us all to starve to death."

With a question on his face, Bobby turned to the elderly Acadian man. "I don't know what happened at Grand Pré back then."

I could tell right away that Bobby was lying.

"I guess I'm too young to know, but I heard they tried starving us out before." To the elderly Acadian woman he said, "At least the Acadians."

The elderly Acadian man said nothing. Neither did the woman.

I knew the answer. I'd experienced it. In 1704. But I said nothing. What could I say? I'd become friends with one of them. He was in our boat right now with us. Sitting beside me. He was the one who took care of the messenger pigeons for the entire west, southwest and southeast coasts and in between of what was now called Nova Scotia, New Scotland. England's promise finally fulfilled.

As our boat floated along with the ingoing tide and the breeze that pushed against its sails, the decaying apugjilu atmosphere settled again. I think even the pigeons felt it as they all seemed to crouch down on their bellies without moving a single feather. Even their breathing was unnoticeable. Had I ever noticed the breathing of pigeons before? Was this atmosphere so tense and dense that I was thinking about how pigeons breathed?

"Hammy," I said. "Are these pigeons the ones who just returned? Won't they be hungry or thirsty? Tired?"

"Heavens, no, Keskoua. I wouldn't do that to any creature. Those who flew back to us are now resting in the community cages. Getting re-acquainted with their friends and relatives, and most importantly, their mates. This is what makes them want to keep returning. Family."

"So these are…?"

"Young ones. It will be their first time away from home. That's why I'm taking them only as far as the village of Chief Jumping Robin. They will return, of course, because they have mates now. But, even so, I don't want their first long-distance adventure to be too daunting for them."

"So that's what makes them want to retu—? Is that a moose, mon cher?" asked the elderly Acadian woman, all excited, and jabbing her elbow into the elderly Acadian man. I now assumed he must be her husband. "It must be. Look how big it is. But there's something wrong with it."

We had just come around into one of the many bays along the way, and there, behind a fence was the biggest horse I had ever seen. Its feet were nearly the size of a person's head. "It's a horse," I said. "I've never seen one so big."

"The Scots brought them with them," Bobby said. "They use them to plow their fields. And to haul the trees away when they cut them down. There will soon be no trees. Nothing left."

Young Bobby seemed to know a lot more about the lives of the Invaders than most people his age. And he was from Île Royale, a territory still held and controlled by France. His French would be perfect. His English was perfect. His Mi´gmaq—or what I'd heard him speak in it—was perfect. Yes, there definitely *was* something about this young man.

The elderly Acadian woman turned to me. "We can't blame the horse for that. Can we?"

"Of course not. It's not the horse's fault what they make them do."

"If I were the horse, I'd run away," said Bobby. "Wait!… He called you Keskoua."

I nodded.

"Are you Keskoua?"

I hesitated.

"The real Keskoua?"

"Is there a false one?"

"I want to talk to you. I've been wanting to meet you. Meet *with* you. Can I? May I? Will you? I mean. That's why I came here. To find you. And look. Here you are. Right here. Isn't that a coincidence."

"Yes," I said. "Quite the coincidence indeed."

"Would it be possible for us to… to talk? I… I… I can't believe it. It's the real Keskoua I'm meeting and talking to."

Hammy laughed. "Just say yes, Keskoua. Don't keep the poor lad flapping his gums in the wind."

"Yes."

"I want to be a storyteller."

I see.

"Like you. Will you teach me how? Please?"

"How can one teach that sort of thing?" asked the nameless man. "It's a gift from God to be able to make up stories. A gift that one has either been given or has not."

"It doesn't work that way," said Hammy. "Keskoua doesn't make stories up. She keeps the history of everybody in her head. Generations of history."

"Impossible!" snorted the nameless man. "That would require high intelligence. These creatures certainly can't manage anything that demanding."

Our captain's laugh was so sudden and loud, it made the pigeons flap in their cages. "You've got a lot to learn about 'these creatures,' stranger. A lot. Do you think *you* can manage something that… Uh. What word did you use? Ah yes. Do you think you can manage something that *demanding*?"

The nameless man snorted again but said nothing more.

"Tell him," said the captain.

I lifted my shoulders and turned back to watch the horse chew at the ground. As we continued along the river, the fence along the shore seemed to follow us.

"I know," said Bobby. "I just don't know how."

"C'est certainement un cadeau," said the elderly Acadian man. "It's definitely a gift. But not a gift for telling stories. No. It's a gift for telling nothing but the truth. Nothing more and nothing less. A gift for remembering exactly how something happened or exactly what and how a person said something, then remembering it for years without changing a single thing."

I turned back around to smile at the elderly Acadian man. "Thank you. Merci."

"But how do you actually do that?" Bobby asked, his eyes moving from the elderly Acadian man to the nameless man and back again. His eyes did not meet mine, I noticed. "It can't be easy." He looked down at his feet. "It can't be easy to always, always, always tell the truth about everything and never ever lie."

"I wouldn't go that far."

Bobby's eyes flicked over to meet mine then flicked away just as quickly. What was he hiding?

"You just don't lie about any of *that*. Meaning the things that happened and who said what. You never add your own opinion to anything. You may have an opinion. And you may voice that opinion—"

"Something our Keskoua does constantly," said Hammy, a big wide smile on his face.

I didn't smile back. "But you cannot ever add that opinion to the history. Or to what another person said."

Bobby drew in a deep breath and held it for a moment before saying, "I guess I'd better start practicing right away. E´e? Yes?"

"E´e."

Six

No one spoke for the rest of our journey along the shores of what was now called the Bay of Fundy. Anytime the English heard our people calling it the Big Bay or the Acadians calling it La Baie fendu—*fendu* meaning split—the English would frown and their noses would get higher. I liked to pretend I couldn't pronounce the French word *fendu* either when I was around them and I called it the Bay of Funny. They didn't think it was *funny*, so of course, that made me do it more often.

Once on shore near Chief Jumping Robin's village, the three of us, Hammy, Bobby and I, quickly set up eight of the pigeon cages on the now-shortened travois. Bobby took the travois handles as Hammy picked up two cages in each hand. I took one cage in each hand.

We'd already sent the extra pigeon back home with the message:

Safely arrived without incident.

Then off we went. I could barely wait to find out why Agada needed to see me. I made suggestions to Hammy and Bobby as to what the problem, or problems, might be. They had no answers to my many questions.

Three excited children met us when we were almost at the village.

"We heard somebody coming," said the girl. I guessed her to be about five years old. She approached Bobby and the travois. "Your pigeons are pretty. The pigeons at our village flew away. All of them. The ones that belong to the people at Hammy's port and the ones from the other ports. Ours flew away, too, but ours came back."

"We heard a lady's voice. Just *her* voice," said one of the boys. He was not much older than the girl.

"That's right," said the other boy, perhaps seven winters old. "Nobody else's voice. Just hers."

The first boy said, "So we thought maybe she was alone and in trouble. That maybe we could help." His face went very serious. "When people are in the bush and they're talking to themselves, it's a bad sign."

At Hammy's laugh, the boys frowned. I managed to keep my mouth shut. The girl was counting pigeons.

"Keskoua doesn't usually need any help. And, as you can see, she's not alone. We're with her." Hammy handed one of his cages to each of the boys then leaned down to face-level and mock-whispered, "Mother Earth told her she should try her best to save everyone else's voice by talking as much as she can."

The boys looked at me, at each other, then back to Hammy.

"Is that true?" asked the girl whose fingers were now inside a cage as she tried to pet one of the pigeons. "Can I carry one of the cages, too?" The pigeon leaned against her fingers.

I set my cages down and pinched my eyebrows together at Hammy as I took the travois from Bobby.

"You'll have to ask Hammy," said Bobby as he adjusted the bag on his back and picked up my cages. "This is the first trip out for these guys. They might be afraid of strangers."

"I'm not a stranger," she tossed back at him. "I live here. Well not exactly right here. I live over there." She pointed through the trees. "You're a stranger. They're not afraid of you. What's your name?"

"You first."

"Je m'appelle Roxane. My name's Roxane."

"I'm Bobby."

"Hey there, Roxie," said Hammy. "How about you help me unload these lads when we get there. How's that?"

"Really?" The young girl turned away and ran off along the path, jumping over tree roots like a lentug, a deer. "Maman, Maman. Hammy dit que je peux aider avec des nouveaux pigeons. Hammy says I can help with the new pigeons. Maman."

***

As I turned the last corner in the path out into the village clearing, I caught sight of Agada running toward us. I set the travois down on the ground as slowly and carefully as I could before I opened my arms and stepped ahead to embrace her. But this was not before I noticed, that while she ran, her dress clung to her, showing a barely rounded belly.

"*Åh, min søde, elskede ven, Keskoua. Hvordan jeg har savnet dig.*"

Agada's hug nearly cracked my ribs. "Easy. I'm a gisigui´sgw. And what did you call me?"

She laughed. "I called you a sweet darling friend and said I missed you. I keep telling you, I'll teach you Danish any time you want. It would save me time translating when I get excited."

"You? Get excited?" It was my turn to laugh. "I know some of your words."

"Those are nasty ones. Don't use those. And you're not an old lady. Stop saying that. Good to see you." She kissed both my cheeks as I kissed hers. "Look at you. Pulling a travois. How can you say you're elderly?"

"They're birds. It's not moose meat or anything."

Agada grabbed my arm. "Come on. I've put water on for tea. Come see my new house."

"House?"

As Agada led me away from the special pigeon-carrying travois, I could hear chatter in the background coming from Hammy and from those he was yelling at.

"What the hell happened? I imagined the entire buildings and structures had been damaged and they are not."

I recognized some of the voices, but not all. I couldn't place the accent of the person who was responding to Hammy's questions. "Somehow your door ended up being left open."

The other voices faded away.

"My door was left open. *My* door? Not *your* door? What kind of caretaker are you if you don't take an interest in these creatures and take ownership of them at least while they are in your care?"

"Well, it wasn't just yours. Er, mine. It's not just your door. Your pigeons. Sorry, it's not only the pigeons from... Not only... the ones from Annap—"

"Out with it!"

"Somehow the doors to... to the other enclosures were... They were left open, too."

"Other enclosures? What other enclosures? There's one for ours and one for yours. What other enclosures?"

Silence.

"He has one in the trees," said a man's voice.

Agreeing mumbles followed his words.

"It's supposed to be secret," said a woman's voice.

I stopped walking to look back. Yes. Hammy was growling at a short man whose clothing mirrored the styles of both Acadia and France. The toque in the man's hands would soon be in shreds if he continued to stretch at it like he was doing. By his accent, I didn't think he was Acadian. Was it French from France? It was hard to tell just by his accent while speaking English. And why would a man from France be here, in this isolated area anyway? Unless... Unless he had come from Île Royale. From Louisbourg. But why?

Hammy sometimes talked loudly and even growled on occasion, yes, but the short man was in no real danger from him. Seeing the way Hammy was reacting to him, though, I wondered what our young, inexperienced pigeons might be thinking. They were watching the goings-on with what appeared to be great interest. I doubted if they would be viewing their new caretaker with trust.

Agada said, "The kettle's on. Let's go."

I turned away. I would ask about the man later.

Hammy's voice continued. "Come on. Help me here. When's the last time this straw was renewed?"

"Yesterday. Sir."

Sir?

"Everything was changed first thing yesterday. Sir. Just before…"

"Hand me another cage."

I couldn't wait until later. "Who is that man?" I asked Agada.

"Never mind him. He came with our new chief. To take a saying from you, 'A fish doesn't come without the bones in it.'"

"Did I really say that?"

"Something like that."

"I think you just made that up."

She slid her arm around mine to hook our elbows. "Maybe I did. Maybe I didn't. Come on."

As the voices of Hammy and the stranger faded behind me, I realized what was different about the village clearing. There were no wikuoms. Only small, square structures made of logs.

"Now I know where all the trees went."

"You should see theirs."

She opened the door to let me enter her cabin.

"Especially the insides of those places. On the other hand, maybe you shouldn't. It would probably make you cry. But, we're trying to go along with what they want. It isn't easy. Trust me when I say that. Not easy at all, at all."

I stepped inside. "No more wikuoms, you mean? They're trying to un-savage us savages?"

"We're determined to keep our buildings small and they're not objecting to that. That's good because there's not as much air to heat up on cold nights."

I always liked it when Agada used the words "we" and "us" when she said anything about our community, about us. It comforted me somehow that choosing this strange young woman to be my friend over twenty years ago had been a good choice. She was one of us.

She pointed to my head. "Is that another gray hair I see?"

"Probably. I'm happy I started to get them when I was young."

"What? Why? I've never heard of that."

"The younger you get gray hairs, the longer you'll live. That's what one of the Grandmothers used to tell me all the time. Look at you. You were born gray. You're going to live forever."

"It's not gray. It's white. And they told me it's white because I did something evil." She laughed. "Superstitions are such nonsense, aren't they?"

I laughed. "Your hair was white long before you did any of *that*."

We both laughed.

"I'm so happy you came out of all of it with your mind intact."

She took the kettle off one part of the stove and set it down on the furthest corner.

"But we have something about *previous* lives in our culture. Did Second Son—"

"Secky."

"Secky. Sorry. Habit. Did Secky ever tell you about that?"

Agada had her back to me as she moved things around on a table at the far wall of the room. The room? The entire house was a single room.

"He said something about… Let me think. Ah, yes. If a child dies young, it's because he wasn't finished with his life in another time but now he was. Is that true?"

"That's what I heard."

"Do you still take sugar in your tea?"

"Nice change of subject, Agada. And a welcome one. Let's stop thinking about death and evil, na to´q?" I put my hand on the back of one of the wooden chairs at the table to caress its wood. It felt nice, smooth. It was shiny. I wondered if it had been made in Montréal like our armoire had been and what flowers its bees might have visited if they'd used beeswax to finish it. "Depends on the tea. Ours or theirs. Ours? Very little sugar. Theirs? As much as you can spare."

I didn't laugh. Neither did Agada.

"It's theirs, I'm afraid. They've fenced off most of the areas where we collect our teas and medicines. They've even cut those plants down. And we can't really get at the maple trees anymore for syrup and sugar. At least not without walking for miles. Thank God for Gracie and Bart Little. They supply me with everything I need and have *ever* needed."

"Me too but I haven't seen them for ages. They're always going here and there."

"You'll get to visit with them this time. They're home." She motioned with her hand. "Sit. Sit. Did you see all those fences on your way here? Empty areas with fences. That's like putting air into a box. To take another saying from you."

"That's not one of mine either. You just made that one up, too."

"You're rubbing off on me." She ran her hand down my arm then placed it against her chest, the place where the heart lives.

"The trees that are left, they've claimed as their own for decorating their yards. Front, back and sides, those vast, empty expanses their huge houses sit in the middle of. They do that in Europe, but why here? It's so beautiful and they're turning it ugly."

I had seen the fences. I'd seen everything and I'd seen the nothing, too. I slumped into the chair.

"I don't understand how they can be so selfish," she said. "The more room they take up, the less room there is for everybody else. Like us. Like the animals we hunt. And fish for, too. They're also taking up land all along the shore now. Did you notice that?"

I didn't want to think about selfish people. I didn't want to get angry. I didn't like being angry. If I could imagine that people were merely uninformed—or even plain unintelligent—I could feel compassion for them. That was more like me. "Speaking of stupid."

"Were we?" She placed a cup and saucer on the table in front of me.

"I will never understand why they want to live in places with square corners. Clean air doesn't get into corners to push out the bad air."

She placed a plate of cookies in the middle of the table. "I've noticed a difference and I haven't even spent a winter in this thing yet."

"Winter. It's been that long since I was last here, hasn't it? Apuknajit, Snow Blinding Month. Six moons since Matuwes went on her Journey."

"She was so happy you came to see her off. It was right after she died they started making their... Shall we call them 'suggestions'? They *suggested* we get rid of our... What did they call our wikuoms? Stacked up rags."

"What a painful ending that poor woman endured. But how could everything have changed so quickly? It's only been a few moons and wikuoms are gone and houses have been built right in the middle of the bush. Or where there used to be bush. I feel sorry for the birds and animals. They've only just recovered from the smoke of the great burning."

"I wouldn't actually call ours houses. They're cabins. No more than that. I like to call mine a house because... Because? There are a lot of reasons."

She poured tea into my cup.

"Wait," I said. "What do they do with all the extra trees they cut down?"

"They sell them to make houses with." She pushed the bowl of sugar toward me. "Or cabins."

I spooned sugar into my cup three times. "Sell them? We don't use money. What do you give them?"

"Our souls?"

I was about to take the first sip of tea while trying desperately not to make a face anticipating the taste of it—the smell was bad enough—when a noise outside saved me. I set the cup down and followed Agada to the window.

Seven

Because of what she was wearing and the state of it, and the blood on her face and on the inside of her exposed leg, I was at first more concerned about the young woman's condition than about who she was.

"Oh my God," said Agada, dashing through the doorway. "Sofia's been assaulted."

"Sofia? That's Sofia?" I was out the door and beside them in an instant.

"Keskoua. What are *you* doing here?" This was followed by an angry glance at her mother.

"What has happened to you?" demanded Agada.

"Nothing, Mother." Sofia smoothed back her hair with one hand and tugged at the front of her torn-open skirt with the other. "Why?"

"Look at you! You're bleeding. Your dress is torn. It's wide open. Your legs are exposed. Blood is dripping down your leg! What happened?"

Sofia moved her hand to the spot above her left eyebrow where the blood was coming from. "Ouch." Her eyes widened when she saw the red on her fingers. "Oh."

"*What? Happened?*"

"Oh. Uh. Chief was there. Robin. Chief Jumping Robin. He—"

At this, Agada rushed away into her cabin.

I put my hand on Sofia's shoulder. "Are you na to´q?"

"Yes, yes. Thanks to Chief Jumping Rob—"

Agada, a pistol in her hand, ran past us toward the center of the village. "*Det er det. Det er det. Jeg har fået nok. Jeg dræber bastarden!*"

"What did she say?"

"She said, That's it. I've had enough. I'm killing the... the..."

"The bastard?"

"Uh. Yes." Sofia's sly glance up at me told me she used the word often but not in front of any of the Grandmothers, like me.

"And she has a weapon. Where did she get the pistol?"

"I think she's always had it."

I reached over and grabbed the waist of Sofia's skirt and whipped it around so the tear would be along the side and no longer exposing the inside of her knees whenever she moved. "Let's go. Keep that side toward me and stay close."

***

I heard banging—cabin doors no doubt—and Agada's loud voice coming through what was left of the trees. "Where is the chief? Where is he? Où est-il? Où est ce morceau de merde? *Hvor er det stykke lort?*"

Clutching her torn skirt together, Sofia ran ahead, calling out, "Mother. *Mor.* Stop it. He didn't do anything bad."

I rounded a cabin to see Agada slamming one of the other cabin doors shut just as a man I knew must be Chief Jumping Robin came from around behind it.

As I said, I had never met him. Nor had I heard much about him. Only that he had been sent here from Île Royale, which was still controlled by France, so he could cause a problem here where we were all trying to "get along" with the English; that those who lived in Île Royale were relieved to see him go; and that those who lived here, in the villages along the eastern side of the Bay of Fundy, rued the day Matuwes, their former chief, had gone on her Journey, leaving an opening for him to move in as chief. I wondered if Bobby knew him. I was certain they had to know each other, both being from the area of Louisbourg. Was that what that "something about Bobby" was? Were these men *en cahute* with each other? Or, "in cahoots" as the Scots pronounced it? Yet another French word gone misheard by Invaders' ears.

Chief Jumping Robin was adjusting the ties around his waist. It appeared he had been out behind the cabin to relieve himself. I hoped he had done this in the special area. I had to assume he had. Like I said, I didn't know him. At all. But by looking at him, how he measured each step as he took it, he seemed to be one of those people who always did everything in a certain way. Their way. The way they had decided everything should always be done, and thinking always that those who didn't do things their way, were fools. His clothing almost gleamed, and he was taking a long time to ensure the ties around his waist were just so.

Then.

"What's going on?" he asked. He did not demand this. He merely asked. I could detect no emotion from him. "I'm here. What's all the racket about? You'll wake the entire bush. Not to mention—" He twirled one of the fingers of his right hand in the air before pointing in the direction of the closest English house. "—them. We don't want that. Do we?"

A crowd had gathered by now and a common voice said, "No, Chief."

"Hell, no," said Bobby stepping up to stand beside Hammy, who was holding one of the pigeons.

It looked like Hammy had been in the midst of showing Roxane, the young girl who had met us on the trail, how to tie a message to a pigeon leg. The pigeon's leg was sticking out from between one of Hammy's fingers, and the young girl was holding a thin piece of birch bark and a length of cedar-bark string. Both Roxane's mouth and the pigeon's mouth were open as they stared at Agada and the chief.

Roxane took the pigeon from Hammy, and cooing at it, walked away toward the pigeons' enclosures.

"What's going on?" asked Chief Jumping Robin. "What are you doing?"

I spoke up. "Agada. *Agada.* Wait."

She whirled, pistol pointing every which way.

"Sofia has something to tell you."

Agada lowered her arm. The pistol's mouth was now pointed to the ground, but Agada's finger was still in the worst spot it could be. I knew that pistols could sometimes make their own decisions.

"Sofia says he was trying to help her."

"Oh, yes. I'm sure that's what he called it." She raised the pistol again, pointing it at Chief Jumping Robin's chest.

It all happened so fast, I'm not sure who did what but the first thing I knew, Bobby was between Agada and Chief Jumping Robin and was trying to take the weapon away from her. A loud bang struck my ears then the stench of gunpowder touched my nose.

Crying out and clutching the side of his chest, Bobby fell to the ground.

Agada gasped. "*Lort!*"

There was no need for me to ask Sofia to translate that word. I knew it well. In several languages. Our word for it was polite: our word translated as excrement.

Both Agada and I rushed to kneel beside Bobby. Someone's hand reached in to grab the pistol from Agada. I think it was the chief himself but I heard Hammy say, "I'll take that, thank you."

"Bobby. Bobby. Can you hear me? Where did it get you?"

Agada was already tearing open Bobby's jacket and rolling it upwards.

"There," she said. "Right there. Let's hope it went all the way through without taking a turn anywhere."

Bobby groaned.

"We have to roll you onto your side," I said.

Bobby nodded.

We rolled him.

He cried out.

By now, we had half the people in the village bending over us like tall trees in a forest.

Agada looked up at them. "Excuse me. Some privacy please?"

The onlookers muttered as they moved away.

"Is he going to be na to´q?" someone asked.

"It went through," said Agada. "He should be fine. We just have to make sure no microbes get inside and grow."

"Who has whiskey?" I called out.

The older of the two boys who had met us on the trail said, "I'll go get some from the Scotsman in the big house over there."

"I'll go with you, Bernie," said the younger boy, whose name was Danny. "But I would ask the woman. Not the man. She's nice."

"Then go," I told them. "As fast as you can."

Eight

Bobby's wound was not serious. The projectile had passed through the side of his chest, barely nicking one of the rib bones, but it would be painful. For weeks.

The boys returned with a small jar of whiskey in no time. I let Bobby hold onto my forearms while Agada poured whiskey onto both sides of his wound. I knew better than to let anyone whose wound was being doused with whiskey to hold my hands. It hadn't happened to me, but I'd seen the results when a soldier had allowed his friend to hold his hands while the friend's broken leg was being reset. The soldier's fingers were unharmed, but the bones in his hands had been crushed to splinters.

Agada and I, with the help of Sofia, managed to get Bobby into Chief Jumping Robin's cabin, and once in there, onto the chief's bed: a real bed, not a cot, and not a twig of cedar anywhere near it, only thick blankets and pillows. Chief Jumping Robin followed us in, directed us, objected to everything we did, but in no way offered help of any kind. And he complained, but in a strange manner, about the blood that was getting all over his bed. I don't think this complaining was actually complaining, it was more like a little baby's whine when it hadn't had enough sleep and didn't know exactly what it wanted, merely that it knew it didn't want what was currently going on. Not knowing the man, I could only suspect he was imagining himself on the bed, his own blood all over it, as though he had been the one shot by Agada.

Like me, Agada always had her munti on her shoulder. I still carried mine even though I wasn't in much demand as a healer anymore. I spent most of my hours working side by side with Mak at our inn. My daughter, Su´n, occasionally—rarely—asked for my assistance or advice. There wasn't much call anymore. Except for one daughter, even her own children had moved away from our village. Neither Su´n nor I had seen them for many years. And we had never met their children. I knew this saddened Su´n to a great degree. It saddened me.

Agada handed Bobby a tiny bottle of reddish-brown liquid. "Drink this."

"What is it?" asked Chief Jumping Robin, who was standing right behind us.

Agada ignored him. "It will relieve most of the pain."

Bobby drank it. "Oh. Ugh. Mah! Terrible. It tastes like…"

"Like *lort*?" said Agada, smiling at him.

"Like mi´jan?" I asked at the same time, trying to hide my smile.

"Worse than that," he said, with his tongue sticking out of his mouth as far as it would go. "It tastes like wolverine piss."

I laughed. "Do you make a habit of drinking wolverine piss?"

"Ooh. Ack. Can you give me something to wash that taste out? And of course not, Keskoua. I was just imagining the worst thing something could taste like."

I found a sweet in my munti. "Here. This should help."

"Thank you." He put the sweet into his mouth. "Ah. Wela´lin. Merci. *Obrigida.* Ah. Yes. That does it. How many other languages can I say thank you in? How about Italian? *Grazie.*"

"You could try Danish. *Tak skal du have,*" suggested Agada. She was hiding neither her smile nor her laughter.

"There's nothing funny about this," said Bobby.

"I'm merely relieved you're not dead by my hand." Agada dug into her munti again and came out with salve. "Grab that bottle from him, will you, Keskoua? Just set it aside for now. I'll sterilize it later."

I took the bottle from Bobby. I could tell he was trying to be as brave as a Brave but he wasn't finding this easy to do.

"Can you hold your arm up a bit more?" she instructed.

"Is that going to sting, too?" Bobby asked her, making his face squeeze together like a little boy might for his first experience of his mother getting burrs out of his hair.

"No." She applied it.

Bobby's face relaxed.

A sliver of light across the floor told me that someone had opened the door. It was Roxane. She stepped inside, her eyes wide while she watched what Agada was doing.

Agada applied moss to Bobby's wound. Front and back, where the projectile had entered and where it had exited.

"You want this now?" I asked, holding out a strip of cloth I guessed she was now searching through her own munti for.

"Thanks." She wrapped the cloth around Bobby, secured it, then helped him lie back onto Chief Jumping Robin's bed.

"Good job you're a little bit fat," said Roxane. "It just took the edge of you."

Bobby groaned. "Don't make me laugh."

Agada tucked everything away into her munti, wrapping the small, used, laudanum bottle in a cloth first. She hooked the munti back over her shoulder, then turned toward her daughter.

"So," said Agada. "Now that we have *that* out of the way."

Sofia was staring down at Bobby as he lay there on the bed. I couldn't tell what was going on inside Sofia's head, but as soon as Agada's fisted hands went to her hips, I knew Sofia could no longer pretend her mother was some ignorable entity. She looked over at me.

I told her to go ahead and tell her mother what had happened. I wanted to know, too.

"I'll tell," said Sofia. "But I want everybody out of here except for *Mor* and Keskoua. Oh, but he can stay, I guess." She pointed at Bobby.

Bobby smiled up at Sofia. "Thank you. I'm not sure I could get up without screaming and that would *really* hurt." To Agada he said, "How long will it take for that stuff you gave me to kick in?"

"Not long," I told him.

Sofia continued, "But I want you to hold your fingers over your ears so you can't hear me."

Bobby laughed. "Ow. I said don't make me laugh." One of his eyes closed and his teeth made the sound water makes when you put it on a smoldering log. He put his hand over the area where his wound was. "You're not serious, are you?"

"I'm as serious as your wound is. And if I catch you listening to me? I'll take my mother's pistol and perforate the other side of you."

Smiling, Bobby saluted, but slowly and carefully. "At least I'd match."

Sofia's eyes did not waver.

"Yes ma'am."

"Everybody out. Out, out," ordered Agada. "You, too, Chief. Go." She flapped her fingers at him.

"But—"

"Go!"

Without smiling, Chief Jumping Robin said, "Yes, ma'am." And out he went, muttering under his breath.

"What happened?"

"You know the red house? The one to the north?"

"Yes."

"Where the gmu´jming grow? The raspberries?"

"Yes."

"I wanted some."

"Continue."

"I wanted some so I climbed over the fence. I went over slow because of those picky things on the top wire."

"Barbs," I said. "It's barbed wire."

"Yes. That stuff. I went to check and see if they were ready yet and they were."

"And?"

"I was eating some. And putting some in my pocket, too." Here, she reached down to where one of her skirt pockets would normally have been, then remembered that I had turned her skirt around. She found it, reached into it. "See?" She showed us a small amount of oozing red stuff with seeds in it. She was about to replace this into her pocket, but paused. "Uh."

From her munti, Agada flipped out a hanky at Sofia. Sofia placed the mess into the hanky, wiped her hand off with it too, then put it into her pocket.

"Then I heard something behind me. Like a snort. And I turned and saw a great big cow running toward me. I ran for the fence but when I tried to climb over it, my skirt got caught and I couldn't get over."

"That would be a bull," I said.

"Like a bull moose? They're crazy. This one was even crazier."

"And?" said Agada.

I glanced over at Bobby who, as he'd promised, had his fingers to his ears but I knew he could hear every word. His mouth was hanging open and I could read the fear and concern for this young woman on his face.

"I cried out and all of a sudden, the chief was there. He had a knife and he cut my skirt away from the picky things. Those barbs. The barbed wire. But the cow was right there and it banged into me and knocked me out of Chief's arms. I fell." She touched her head. "I hit a rock but I was sort of on top of Chief so it didn't hurt as much as it could have. That's what he said anyway."

"Then how did you get the blood on your leg?" demanded Agada.

She was holding herself so tensely, I thought she might shatter.

"From the cow. Its horn got me. I got another scratch on the top of my leg at the back, too. From the barbed wire." She turned to lift her skirt to show us.

"That must hurt," said Bobby from the bed.

"I'm na to´q," she answered. Then, "Hey. You're not supposed to be listening."

"I'm not so sure you should be showing me your bare bottom, either."

With a *huff* and a reddening face, Sofia stomped out of Chief Jumping Robin's cabin.

"You satisfied with that story?" I asked Agada.

"It's crazy enough to be true. Come with me," she said, and we stepped out of the cabin. She took my arm. "You don't have much time before the tide starts going out and you have to go back home. And we have to talk."

I pointed to her slightly rounded belly. "About that?"

"That, too."

Nine

"I know it's a difficult age for young people," Agada said as we moved to the corner of the chief's cabin where we could watch for eavesdroppers along two of the outside walls. "But there's more going on with Sofia than that. I think that only makes it more difficult for her." We stood facing each other so we could watch into the trees behind us, too. We spoke quietly.

"What's going on with her then? Your message sounded urgent."

"Urgent for her and urgent for something else, too. But for her, it's the chief. It's Chief Jumping Robin who's causing all the extra anxiety in her life."

"She's not the only one," came Bobby's quiet voice from the cabin doorway. "He gave us all grief." He came slowly through the doorway. "I have to…" He pointed behind the cabin. "… relieve myself."

"You know him?"

"Of course, I do. He's from Île Royale, too. Louisbourg."

"What?" Agada said. "I mean, I knew he was from there, but you are, too?"

"I came here to find Keskoua. I decided my best plan…" Bobby squeezed up his face and touched his side. "Ow. I assumed he would have heard of her. He would probably know where to find her. I knew where to find him at least. Ow."

"And were you right?"

"In a roundabout way, I suppose."

Agada stepped to Bobby's side and raised his jacket to check his wound. "May I ask you something?"

"Sure. Easy. Easy."

"Where did the name Jumping Robin come from?"

"E´e. Yes. I want to know, too," I said.

Bobby laughed and gasped at the same time. "You guys are so cruel. Make me laugh all the time."

"You know?"

"It's because he can't dance. He just kind of… hops. On two feet."

Before I let my laugh escape, I glanced around through the trees to see if Chief Jumping Robin was anywhere near us. I didn't see him.

Bobby waved at us over his head as he cautiously made his way around the far side of the cabin toward the relief area.

"He follows her everywhere."

"He does? Why?"

"It appears to be one thing but it also appears to be another. That's one of the main reasons she wants to leave."

"Leave?"

"She says he makes her skin itch. Nothing feels right, she says."

"From what I've already heard and seen, he would make mine more than itch."

"She says some of the young men like her and always seem to show up where she goes. But she says it doesn't feel the same. Not at all. She says it isn't like that when he follows her. It's like he's making mental notes. How did she put it? 'Like just before you start to carve up a moose.'"

"Has he ever harmed her? Has he ever forced himself on her? Done anything inappropriate?"

"She says no and I believe her. But he's just always there. Right there."

"Why doesn't she tell the Grandmothers about this? They could speak with him."

"They're part of the problem."

"How?"

"He has no woman. He is well over thirty years old. Between you and me, I think it's because he's always interfering with everybody else's business so doesn't have time for anything else. Not even time for fun on the cedars. But I like to give everyone the benefit of the doubt."

I frowned. "There are times when that doesn't apply, you know. I don't like him. I don't like to not like someone, but it usually ends up that there's a good reason. So I go with my feelings."

"I'm getting better at that. I still need more practice, but I think there's hope." She smiled. "Anyway, the Grandmothers are the ones who recommended—at a Sacred Fire, no less, so practically sacrosanct, and they all agreed—that he should find himself a woman, a wife, and wouldn't dear young Sofia fit that requirement perfectly."

"So he thinks he now has the right to follow her around everywhere? Doesn't Sofia have anything to say about it?"

"Of course she does and the Grandmothers know that and agree. It's him. I don't think he understands any of it. I don't think he's even operating on instinct. I think it's more just going through the motions. Doing what he thinks he should be doing when it comes to… romance. Romance? I don't think he has a single speck of understanding where love is concerned. Makes my skin both itch *and* crawl. What do you think, Keskoua? Could she perhaps go back with you? Get a position at your inn. My sister could teach her how to cook. And if Sofia isn't here, I would know for sure if he's only stalking *her*. I have a feel—"

I interrupted her. "It's not up to Mak and me anymore. We're moving to Mirligueche." I ignored her gasp. "Zeke and Solange are taking over. Sofia would have to ask them. I can't imagine Zeke would object to Solange's niece coming there to work, though. I mean, he knows Sofia. He likes her. And Solange. Well, Sofia *is* her niece and I know she loves her dearly."

Agada's voice rose to its normal pitch. "You're what? Moving to Mirligueche? Since when? And when?"

"As soon as I get back. Everything's already been shipped. Even Mak. Everything but me."

I laughed. Agada didn't.

"But why?"

"Our new inn. It's built. The furniture is on the way and will soon be there. I'm surprised you didn't know all this." I paused. "Or... Maybe it's because I was so excited about it and got so caught up in it, I forgot to tell you. I'm sorry. Our new inn is almost ready for patrons. As soon as we get there, we'll open. J-B is overseeing everything in spite of everything *else* that's going on in that man's life. I don't know how he does it."

Just then Sofia appeared from inside the trees and a shadow told me that Chief Jumping Robin was hiding there behind a tree, watching her. Us? Had he heard what we'd been saying about him? About Sofia and the possibility of her going away?

"Oh. That would be even better!" Sofia said. "Do you need help at the new place? I could work there. Make money. It's closer to Boston there. I want to go to Boston and live there. I've heard that Boston is nice."

"Um. Yes. I could talk this over with Mak. How about I do that and let you know? But Boston? Boston is nice. But Boston is very different. And it's the last place a young woman of your age—and your lack of experience with the outside world—should ever be alone in. Take my word for that." I turned back to Agada. "You were about to say something."

"Ah, there you are. We heard that a young man has been injured." A familiar voice told me that Little Bat had arrived. "Can we help?"

Little Gracie and Little Bat were now a couple, and had been for many years. They called themselves The Littles. Gracie Little and Bart Little.

The English accepted that as far as their names went, but not as far as anything else went. Gracie was Mak's niece and just as dark-skinned as he was, if not more so because she spent most of her time outdoors. Little Bat's skin would hardly pass the Invaders' test of White either, he was one of our people. Their children's skin colors ranged everywhere in between.

They acknowledged my presence with words and warm hugs, but when Bart took a package from his munti, opened it and showed it to Agada, the three of them huddled together like swallows in a rainstorm, leaving me standing there alone.

I hadn't heard him approach, but Bobby was at my ear. "I see you aren't busy. Good. Someone wants to talk to you. They're near the relief area.

"You're na to´q?"

"I am. The medicine has taken hold."

I slipped away.

***

The young girl who had taken such an interest in Hammy's pigeons was waiting for me behind a very old and broad oak tree.

"Roxane. What is it? Is everything na to´q? Ça va bien?"

"I know who let all the pigeons go," she said, her voice barely more than a whisper. "And please call me Roxie. The only ones who call me Roxane are my parents."

"Roxie it is then. Do you want to tell me?" I'd heard secrets from children before and didn't usually like what they told me. They didn't usually like telling their secrets, either. It often meant breaking a promise. Sometimes a promise that included keeping a loved one alive. Like, *Don't tell anyone or I'll kill your sister. Your mother. Your brother. Your father.*

"I already know that some secrets should never be secret," Roxie said. "So you don't have to look at me like that, all sad and worried. Agada told me all about that sort of thing. This isn't one of those. This one isn't a bad secret. This secret is an important one to keep as a secret but I don't like having secrets." She stepped closer to me but turned her face away. "It feels like I'm a messenger pigeon with a stone on its leg instead of just a little piece of birch bark."

"That would make it difficult for the poor wee pigeon. Wouldn't it?"

"It wouldn't be able to fly right."

"No. It wouldn't."

"Maybe it wouldn't even be able to walk. To get to its food, you know?"

"That's right. Maybe not."

"It makes me not want to talk to anybody anymore. At all. In case any words come out accidentally. I have to keep quiet even if it makes the word-maker in my throat rot away from disuse."

I bit my tongue to stop myself from smiling. A word-maker rotting away from disuse would never be a problem with me and I had a feeling, just then, that it wouldn't be for Roxie in the future, either.

"In case… You know. In case…"

"In case the stone falls off and injures someone if the pigeon does happen to get into the air?"

"Exactly." Her eyes met mine. "Agada's the one who let the pigeons out." Her eyes turned downward. "All of them. Ours. Yours. And… And theirs. Theirs that come and theirs that go to and from way back in the trees. The ones Guillaume puts messages on and takes messages off."

Theirs. So that's what the unfamiliar pigeon caretaker… Guillaume, it was… had been talking about. Or trying not *to talk about.* "Oh." I tried not to show surprise on my face even though she wasn't looking at it right then. Surprise had already come out of my mouth so it didn't matter anyway. No rotting word-maker in this throat.

"Guillaume comes from a place called France and the messages are about our young men. Where they are. Where they go. How many of them are in the village. How many aren't. If they're fishing. If they're not.

If they're selling the fish. If they're not. They want to know how many of us little ones there are, too. And where we go to play. Why would they want to know all that?" She looked into my eyes again. This young girl was making me unable to hide behind my face more than anyone had every managed before. "Do you think she'll be angry with me? For telling you?"

"I don't think so, sweet girl. Agada and I are very good friends. I know there's something she's wanting to talk to me about. We already talked about one thing. And I know there's another. I think maybe this is it."

"There's more."

I said nothing. I just moved my head the slightest bit to tell her to go ahead. If I pushed her, if I asked any question, I might send her off like a frightened apalqaqamej, a frightened chipmunk. She was already looking around in every direction.

"*She* has a great big, huge boulder on her leg. And it's got to do with the secret in her belly." Once again, Roxie's eyes averted mine to search the trees behind me. A shy smile bloomed on her face when her eyes returned to mine. "We all know there's a baby in there, but I'm the only one who knows who put it in there." Her smile went away. "And where he is. And it's a great big, huge secret that I can't tell anybody. If they find him, they'll take him away and kill him."

"Maybe we should move back toward the village? To an open spot. Where we won't have to be constantly watching what might be behind all the trees around here?"

She shrugged and glanced around again. And she kept looking behind me which made me extra nervous.

"Are you afraid there might be a chenoo around?"

"I'm not afraid of chenoos," she said. "They're not real. But if you're worried about Chief Jumping Robin following me around like a chenoo, and maybe hurting me, and that's why you're saying that, don't worry about that, either. He doesn't know I know anything. I'm 'just a child.' Nobody pays attention to 'just a child.'"

Once again, I tried to hide my feeling behind my face. This time, my guilt feeling.

"You see, he's always telling everybody he's in love with Sofia. Like, you know, when anybody asks why he's always around her. He's a dirty, rotten liar." Roxie reached out to grab the front of my jacket, so she could pull me down closer toward her. "He follows Agada more than he follows Sofia."

"App? What?"

"He's just pretending he's in love with Sofia. You know. So nobody will find out his real… What's that word? Uh…"

"His real motive?"

"That's it. That's the word. He has real motive. A scary motive. Two scary motives."

"Hey," came Agada's voice from behind me. "What are you girls up to?"

"I could ask you the same question," I said.

Ten

Back at Chief Jumping Robin's cabin, we found Bobby standing outside, talking with the Littles. Gracie Little was the only one facing me. When she saw me, she greeted me loudly. "Keskoua. How are you?"

Their conversation stopped like a canoe hitting a submerged log. Bart Little and Bobby turned to face me. Their lips were smiling but their eyes weren't.

"Where's the chief?" I asked.

"Gone somewhere," Bart said. "Find Sofia and you'll probably find him."

"Bobby?" I said. "Go find him and distract him. Keep him away. Agada and I have something private to discuss."

"We know," said Gracie Little. "And that's a good idea."

"I'll go with Bobby," said Roxie. "That way, if anybody…" When she said the word *anybody*, she paused and made her eyes and her mouth go wide. "… if anybody sees us, they'll think I'm showing him around. And I can ask the anybody what else I can show to this stranger. And I can pretend I don't know where that is. So the anybody will have to come with us."

When Gracie Little's eyes met mine, they told my eyes and mine told hers how impressed we were at hearing such wisdom from so young a child.

"Is that not na to´q?" Roxie asked, frowning up at our faces.

"It's very much na to´q," I said. "Run along, you two."

"Run?"

"You know what I mean, Bobby."

Eleven

"Very well," said Agada. "I'll tell you. But some of what I tell you will have to be lies."

"I see."

"In fact, much of what I tell you will be lies. You'll have to discern the truth out of it yourself. Or. Perhaps it's better you don't at all."

Standing with us, the Littles nodded.

"Most of it," Agada added.

"I'm assuming this is in case I'm captured and tortured?"

"That's not funny."

"It is so," said Bart Little, smiling wide. "Keskoua always makes me laugh." The look from Agada removed his smile instantly. "Sorry."

"After Matuwes left on her Journey and Chief Jumping Robin came to our village, I… Come to think of it, he was already here when she… I guess nobody paid any attention to him. We were all too concerned about Matuwes to notice him. He was always in the background. Quiet. Hmm. Anyway, I went to where the boats come in and out for passengers. You know, to the Big Bay. Where you came in. Where everybody comes in and out when they visit us."

Why was she telling me things I already knew?

"I found someone. A man. He'd been washed up on shore. He appeared to have been drowned. He was barely conscious.

"'Help me,' he said. 'I cannot be seen.'

"I took him to the cave near there. Do you know the one I mean?"

I shook my head. As far as I knew, there were no caves anywhere near that area.

"He's a Scotsman," Agada continued. "He told me to call him Ian." She was making no eye contact with me at all. She was looking at somewhere below my chin.

Even though I knew this was most likely a serious situation, I couldn't help myself. I wanted her to feel at ease. I said, "I thought it was only in Ireland that handsome lovers got washed up on shore."

"What?" said Bart Little. "Men are washed up on shore in Ireland on a regular basis?"

"She reads a lot of books," offered Agada. "Love stories. I think she's trying to be funny again." To me, she said, "May I continue?"

Smiling, Bart Little nodded. "See what I mean? She's funny."

A glance from Agada removed Bart Little's smile again but not completely.

"I offered to care for him. To bring him food and water while he recovered. He'd been on a pirate ship and it had gone down."

I laughed. "This is the part that's a lie, right? I've not heard of pirate ships for years. Either floating or sinking. The laws are too strict now. It takes either a very brave or a very desperate man to pirate a ship. Or an unintelligent one. It's a good way to get yourself hanged."

Agada closed her eyes at me. "Making things up isn't easy for me, Keskoua. Bear with me, please. When I found out I was being followed by…" Agada turned her head from one side to the other, looking everywhere, like an owl might—except not all the way around like an owl could. "When I found out I was being followed by him, Gracie and Bart offered to help me look after Ian. But they are often away. It wasn't easy. I made certain I always brought enough water to last for many days, in case I was followed. I didn't dare risk exposing his hiding place. But food was different. I left him with a supply of pemmican for the times I could not get to him with fresh. He doesn't like it but says… How did he put it? 'It's better than death but only by so much.'"

I had the same opinion of pemmican. I was sure I could like this man.

Gracie Little spoke up. "For some reason… Right, Agada? For some reason, Chief Jumping Robin is anxious to know where he is, isn't he? Should you not be telling this part to Keskoua? To ensure she doesn't say the wrong thing to the wrong man?"

"He knows about this Scotsman?"

"We don't know for certain what he knows or how he knows it, even if he does," said Agada. "We suspect. That's all. To prevent us from taking any chances. We are hoping, that like everything else, he only thinks he knows something. Although he does know something about—Uh! No. Sorry."

"And we want to keep it that way," said Bart Little, each word spoken with strength.

"We cannot ever let him find Ian." Agada's hand went to her belly.

"No, we cannot," said Gracie and Bart Little as one.

"I love him."

"No lie there," said Gracie Little. "That she does. But the baby is definitely an unfortunate turn of events."

"When the baby is born, of course we'll be considered, by our people, to be married," said Agada. "I have no problem with that and neither does Ian."

"But the English will expect to know who the father is," said Bart Little. "So he can be named and recorded as such. Because Agada is not Mi´gmaw. She was born in Ireland. So by them she is considered to be… Dare I say it? She is considered to be 'human,' so important enough to be remembered on paper. The English will force them to be properly married in one of their churches. He'll be found out."

Agada now had both hands on her belly. "If he's found out, he'll be hanged. That part is true."

From the other side of the clearing came Hammy's voice: "Where the hell is sh—? There you are. Come on. Let's go. I've convinced the captain to wait." Hammy grabbed my arm and as he dragged me along with him, he continued. "Sofia and Bobby are already on board. As are the pigeons were taking. Hurry. Where have you been?"

"Wait!" Agada was running alongside us almost instantly. "Sofia is already on board? On board what?"

"The boat. The boat taking us to Annapolis Royal. Why?"

"*WHY?*"

"She said you know. She said she has your permission to go with us to Annapolis Royal. Then she'll go along with Keskoua to Mirligueche. She said she has acquired a position there with Mak and Keskoua at their new… their… their new inn… Why are you ladies looking at me like that?"

By now, we had reached the far edge of the village and were about to head into the path that would lead us to the shore where one of the boats waited for Hammy and me. Agada was still with us and not the slightest bit out of breath. I couldn't say the same for myself.

"She's going? And she didn't even hug me goodbye?" Agada had stopped running alongside us.

"Come with us then," called Hammy back to her. "You can say goodbye to her if you're quick about it. This captain is a good man, albeit an impatient one, but he won't cast off until you at least exchange hugs with your daughter. Come with us. Agada. Come on."

***

Agada and Sofia's goodbyes were quick and full of love and with not a little amount of tears running down their cheeks.

Hammy cast off for the captain and away we went with both the wind and the tides in our favor.

As we caught the current at the bend of the shore, I looked back. I thought I saw a shadow come out of the trees to put an arm around Agada. The shadow and Agada embraced. That part of the story was true then. There *was* a man, possibly a Scotsman, possibly a man who said she could call him Ian, and this Ian was possibly hiding. But why? And from whom?

And I hadn't had a chance to ask her why she had let all the pigeons loose. Maybe it was not that I hadn't had a chance, maybe I didn't want to know. Between what Agada had said and hadn't said, and from what little Roxie had told me, the Scotsman, Ian, was probably not the only one in grave danger.

***

On the return trip by water to the area of Annapolis Royal, Bobby did not suggest we play games about finding animals, plants and birds along the shoreline; he slept the entire way. Sofia, stitching together her ripped New England skirt with needle and thread I'd had in my munti, sat silent at the bow end of the boat and cried the entire way. I don't know how she could see to work. Hammy and the captain chatted about nothing the entire way. And for the entire way, I tried to imagine what my new life in Mirligueche would bring. Little did I know.

Twelve

Our trip overland toward Annapolis Royal and a ship was slow. I was amazed at Bobby's ability to control (ignore?) the pain he must have been feeling every time he breathed, but despite this inner strength of his, he was unable to keep up a normal pace. Sofia and I took turns carrying the pigeon travois with Hammy.

When we arrived at the port, Bobby sat down immediately on the dock, water pouring out of his forehead, and breathing fast but not deeply. I handed him a hanky but he was barely able to lift his arm to wipe his face.

Hammy had run on ahead to check on boarding time and to go to the inn to collect enough shillings to pay for two extra passengers: Sofia and Bobby. Yes, Bobby would be coming along. He had insisted. He had also said he had enough money to pay for his own fare, but Hammy had insisted, too. Hammy had won the argument.

To me, Bobby said: "I came here to find you, didn't I? And I found you. Why would I let you go on ahead? All that trouble for nothing?"

I wasn't sure what to think of that. I both believed him and didn't.

"Besides," he added. "You're the one with the medicine that kills my pain. I would follow you anywhere."

Just as Hammy returned to where the three of us were waiting, a man carrying several cages packed full of messenger pigeons waddled past. He had just deboarded the ship we would be leaving on. Was he walking like that because of an injury? He did not appear to have a damaged leg as his waddle was even. Were the cages heavy? No, they were made of cedar wood, as ours were. And pigeons weigh nothing.

"That man must have come all the way from Boston," I said. "Looks like he's got sea legs." I knew what that felt like. I'd gone to Boston by sea. Many years ago.

Hammy called out to the man. "Hey, there. Want a hand with those?"

The man carrying the cages turned to face Hammy with a grateful smile but when his eyes went to where Bobby was sitting, the man quickly moved his face away from us and muttered something that sounded like, "I'm quite fine. Quite fine. Thank you. I'm quite fine." As he picked up his pace, he almost lost his balance.

"I don't recognize those pigeons," said Hammy. "Nor their caretaker. They're not ours. And they're not from Mirligueche, either. They have too much white on them."

"You can tell the difference between pigeons?" I asked.

"Most certainly. Ours all have black heads and dark gray bodies. Didn't you see that? The ones from Mirligueche have lighter-gray bodies and more white sprinkled throughout. The ones that lad is carrying are almost pure white in the body. I'm surprised you didn't notice the difference."

I hadn't. But I promised myself I would in future.

"Our pigeons, and those of our friends, Flower Stalk and Agada, have varying undersides. I have names for some of them." He glanced at me. "But I don't like to name them. They don't live forever, you know."

"I recognize that man," whispered Bobby. "He's French."

"French?" said Hammy. "He's dressed rather fancily for an Acadian."

"Louisbourg. France French."

"Oh." *Interesting. Another one. Pigeons and pigeons and French from France. Very interesting.*

***

In no time, I was on a ship and sitting in a cabin below decks, talking with Bobby who was asking when he would be able to drink his next bottle of laudanum and I was telling him he could have only one per day and only for four days. That he had at least three hours to go for the second of these bottles.

"When those four days are done, you are going to need every ounce of willpower you have within you."

He slumped back against the cushions on his cot. "I suspected so. That stuff feels too good to be something one can take all the time. I've heard of those who become tied to medicines. I've heard it can be an even worse situation than being tied to alcohol."

"I've heard that too. But now that I have you in my power… as it were…"

He didn't seem to think my comment was as funny as I did.

"I would like to hear—"

He cut my words off. "I know. You want to know the real reason I wanted to go to that area of Acadia. Ah. Excuse me, Nova Scotia."

"Talk," I said.

He began.

"I was born in Chedabucto so we visited Île Royale all the time, as far up the coast as Louisbourg. Now that I think about it, we always went as far up the coast as Louisbourg. I don't think we ever stopped in between."

I could almost see the thoughts bouncing around in his head.

"And those from Île Royale visited us. Now that I think about it, it was always those from Louisbourg. It's amazing how little we see going on when we're young, isn't it? I'm surprised I don't have a France French accent, then. That's all I ever heard."

"You do," I said. "But only slight so not annoying."

"What? Ow. Don't make me laugh."

"The English are just as bad if you mispronounce one of their words. Go ahead. Let it out. Laughter is good for healing."

"So you say." Once again, his teeth made the sound of water on hot coals. "Anyway. We were watched carefully by the English when we were on this side of the strait, so eventually, to avoid all that uncomfortable scrutiny, we moved to Louisbourg permanently. I was around nine years old when we moved."

"Which side are you on then?" I asked him.

"Which side indeed? I'm on side of the Mi´gmaq. And the side of the Acadians. Why would I not be? I am half and half."

"Which direction?"

"Mi´gmaw mother, Acadian father." Here, he adjusted himself on the pillows. "How many hours left?"

"Still three."

"I am Mi´gmaw back through as many mothers as I can count. Mother, grandmother, great grandmother and her mother, too." He smiled. "It seems all my female ancestors liked Acadian men because all the fathers in me are Acadian as far back as when they first came here. Like I told you, I'm half and half."

"Not quite," I said, but I added nothing more. He was half and half by tradition. By blood, much more Acadian.

"I try to let the French believe I'm on their side and the English that I'm on theirs. But I'm on neither."

I didn't ask him how he managed to do that. I wanted him to keep talking. Perhaps this was what that *something about him* was, his ability to deceive.

"The English obviously distrust any of us with French blood."

I nodded agreement.

"And the French expect those with French blood to be on their side."

Not too long ago, I had thought the French and the Acadians were one and the same. But it appeared, from what I had seen and heard with my own eyes and ears, especially lately, that the French and the English were the ones who were the same. They each wanted control over the other and would kill each other to get what they wanted. And kill anybody in their way. Like us. And the Acadians.

"They want the Acadians to choose a side. Those who don't are thought of as treasonous. Treasonous in the minds of the French and treasonous in the minds of the English."

"The Acadians I know don't want to fight with anyone," I said. "And won't. They want to be left alone to go about their own business."

"That's where Ian comes in."

"Ah. You know about him."

"I do."

"Agada said Ian's a Scotsman. So he's already on one side. The side of the English."

"Do you know the Guédrys?"

"Of course I do. They're like family to me."

"One of the sons refused to sign the Treaty. I'm talking about the Treaty of Utrecht. The one everybody signed in 1713, promising they wouldn't fight against England. At least everyone was supposed to sign."

"You're talking about Pierre. Claude and Marguerite's son."

Bobby nodded.

"Marguerite told me about it. Almost every Acadian signed only to keep the English from constantly bothering them to do it. From constantly following them around expecting them to... I don't know. Expecting them to—"

"Blow something up?" offered Bobby.

"The Guédrys are a peaceful, agreeable lot. They wouldn't be doing anything like that. According to Marguerite, Pierre was insulted by their demands and that's why he refused to sign. She told me 'He refused to sign out of principle.' But he was sixteen winters old then. Boys of your age can be difficult. Stubborn. Look at you. You aren't bowing down to anyone either. You… Oh. Sorry."

Bobby's mouth was smiling at me. His head was tilted. "I'm almost eighteen. He was only sixteen. There's a difference."

"There is. And I am happy to see that you have realized how much trouble a young man can get into by making decisions like that. Decisions that can affect your whole life and that of your family. Forever maybe."

"Is it too late for him to sign at least something? Can he sign the June peace treaty? I know he's Acadian, not Mi´gmaw, and not even mixed, just his wife is, but couldn't he still sign something? For the sake of her and the children?"

"I'm not so sure he would. By refusing to sign back then, he made a commitment. When a Guédry commits to anything, they stick to their word."

"So *not* giving your word is giving your word?"

It sounded strange put that way, but Bobby was right. "He needs to balance keeping his word with getting his wife and children off that houseboat."

"Were you aware they're at the mercy of the *children* of their friends now?"

"What? No." I'd heard nothing of this.

"The guards had gotten so watchful and strict, they weren't missing a thing that the adults did anywhere near his houseboat. People could no longer pass them food and water without finding themselves at the wrong end of a musket barrel."

"No. No. You're not telling me that children are coming to the docks now."

Bobby said nothing and his face didn't change.

"No. No. He needs to accept that he made a mistake. He needs to sign something. Anything. Now! They can't have children in places where they'll be noticed. Especially Mi´gmaw children. They're even taking the mixed now, too, and selling them as… as…"

Bobby didn't finish my sentence for me and I'm glad he didn't. I didn't like that word coming out of my mouth or going into my ears.

"But I still like and respect him," said Bobby.

I said nothing. I was reeling with worry.

"Did you know they're calling him LaBine now?"

I didn't.

"It means The Hoe. Because he doesn't farm anymore. The Acadians are doing it to be mean. They're trying to make him change his mind. He's causing not only his family trouble, but anyone who works on the docks or sells their products there."

I had to lighten the air around me. My stomach was tightening up and my head was telling my braids they were too tight. That was one thing about myself I don't think I could or would ever change. *When things are bad, make a joke.* "I think La Poisson would be a better name, don't you?"

"La Poisson? The Fish? What are you talking about?"

"He lives on the water. I'm surprised his boys weren't born as fish. And little Josephe-Marie as a mermaid."

Bobby adjusted himself on the pillows again. "He has another child on the way."

"I know. He needs to sign something and accept England as his ruler."

"Are we sure he can't sign the June treaty? J-B signed it. He's not Mi´gmaw either. Did you know about that one?"

"I signed that one. All the Mi´gmaq in our area did. Most of the Acadians signed in support of us. We're all family despite what the English say and think."

"Maybe if he at least signed that one, it could help get J-B's son… uh… out of prison faster. Or from wherever he is." Bobby's face told me nothing about his thoughts. "You know. Just start cooperating with them on every matter. Show them—"

"Show them constant smiles and say yessah massah we won't fish in *'your'* waterways anymore? We'll stop feeding fish to our families? And deer and moose, too? What will we be left with? Eating stones? And if we did, they'd probably find a way to make money from stones and forbid us to use them on top of everything else."

Bobby smiled with kindness and shifted positions again. "I think you already know this, but I'm going to tell you that J-B's son and the others who went missing along with him are not in a Boston prison. The Littles have been to Boston and they said those children are nowhere near the prison there. None of the ones taken from here are."

It was true then. The whispered rumors I'd heard were true. I wanted to take a side path off the one Bobby was heading down. I did not want my mind to go into that forest, off that cliff onto the rocks of mental pain below. I'd seen with my own eyes what traders did to slaves. I'd heard even more from my husband, Mak, who'd experienced it himself. He still woke in the middle of the night sometimes, sweating with fear. No. I did not want—in the slightest—to imagine what J-B's young son could be experiencing. I asked, "How well do you know the Littles?"

Once again, I knew Bobby knew what was in my mind. He allowed me to set the subject of slavery aside. "I know them well."

"Why then do I not know you."

"Perhaps you do."

This young man was definitely a mystery. He resumed.

The Scotsman, Ian, had been brought to the area of Chief Jumping Robin's village by Gracie and Bart Little. I hadn't had to ask Bobby why there. The Littles had brought him there because that village was their home and they knew everyone; they knew whom they could trust and whom they could not. The Scotsman, Ian, had suffered no injury. He had not been nearly drowned. He was on the run. On the run from the noose.

"As you are well aware, there are five points of view," Bobby said.

"At least five. The English, which includes the Scots, of course. Us. And by 'us' I mean those of us who are pure which is you and not me; and those of us who are mixed which is me and not you. The Acadian French, meaning the Catholics. And the France French. France wants to reclaim the land they lost to England, and by any means they can. The English want to keep the land they took from the French, and by any means they can. We are in the middle so at the mercy of both sides. All sides."

He paused.

I waited.

"I got sent by those at Fort Louisbourg to spy on someone."

"And are you spying?"

"If I were or I weren't, I wouldn't be allowed to tell you, would I?"

"The noose?"

"Most likely the firing squad. But I am not spying. I refuse to spy. Like I told you, I am on neither side but must pretend I'm on both. Without having them catch on to me. That's the real reason I went to the village of Jumping Robin. *Chief* Jumping Robin. I was not looking for you. I knew it was you the moment I laid eyes on you at the docks, but I needed a reason to go there. You were an excuse."

"Oh. Well. Thank you for letting me know. Happy to be of service."

"Do you realize that when you are saying something you don't mean, your eyebr—" He smiled. "Never mind. At first my question was why do they want me to spy on him, of all people. He's a… He's a nothing. They told me he had been sent by them, by Louisbourg, to spy on the English. This surprised me, too, as he doesn't seem to be capable of anything requiring a skill like that. But I soon learned that he is actually working for the slave traders. He is providing them with information about the young people in his area. So they can capture them, too. It's getting more and more dangerous for everyone, everywhere. And J-B is right in the middle of it."

"J-B because of his son. Yes?"

"It's beyond that now. He's getting too close to the truth with all his questions not only about where his son and young brother-in-law are, but where the other children and young Mi´gmaw boys—mostly boys—are going. But since he signed that treaty in June, he is wary. Very wary. Because even though he has fulfilled his side of the agreement by signing the treaty of peace between the Mi´gmaq and the English, his son is still nowhere to be seen. They haven't produced him as promised. J-B is in turmoil. He knows. He knows where the young Mi´gmaq are going. He knows full well but his mind refuses to accept it. And worse, if he lets slip that he knows, he will be set up.

"Need I say that those at Louisbourg are therefore not trusting J-B? For one thing, they don't want him bringing anything to light lest it cause an escalation of problems. They do not want any kind of attention drawn to the areas where the boys are being taken from. Because…" Bobby's voice lowered. "Can you keep a secret?"

"Of course."

"Spies from Louisbourg are everywhere. So if attention is drawn to the areas where the children are disappearing from, there might be those who look more closely at this and that. Do you know what I'm saying?"

This was very serious and complicated. I hadn't realized just how complicated. How serious.

"The New Englanders are taking these young native boys as slaves. Slavery is discouraged by a large number of people in Massachusetts. Religious groups who hold sway. So where are they sending them?"

There. He said the word. The word I didn't want to say or hear. *Slavery*. Slavery meant slaves. People. Had these slavers reached our land now, too?

"They're saying J-B has sided with England by signing that agreement." Bobby shifted again. "How much longer?"

"Two and a half hours."

"I know J-B. I know Pierre. I like them both. I like their wives. I like their children. I'm very concerned about them all because *both* the French and the English are plotting to get rid of both Pierre and J-B. They were hoping to catch at least one of them going against their agreement. Or non-agreement in Pierre's case, I guess. I've even heard rumors that one of the men at Louisbourg is planning to force J-B to comply with *their* wishes and take the side of the French, despite the peace treaty he agreed to. The man at Louisbourg plans to do this by kidnapping more of the local Mi´gmaw children. He will claim that J-B is behind this."

I dug into my munti. "I want a sweet. Do you?"

"I'll save mine for… What is it now? Two hours?"

"It's still two and a half. Sorry, Bobby."

"What Raymond plans to do is keep the children in Louisbourg and threaten to turn them over to the English for treason if J-B does not agree with Raymond's demands. He says J-B is… How did he put it? 'J-B—and LaBine—are setting the Acadians against the French.'"

"They aren't setting anyone against the French. Or against the English either," I said. "What are they talking about? That so-called peace treaty we signed is about the fishing industry."

"Ah yes. The great New England fishery business. Money, money, money. As if they can't spare a few fish for those who fish only to eat and feed their families." Bobby shrugged. "Ow. Yes. I will take that sweet after all. But wait. Do you have another for later? To get that foul taste out of my mouth?"

"I do." I handed him the sweet.

"What Raymond really plans to do after he takes the children, I do not know. I imagine he will do them no harm. But Raymond is… Let's say he did not get to his high position at the fort by being kind to others."

"How will he be able to take these children? Surely it's busy enough in Mirligueche, with guards and people everywhere and ships and passengers and fishers going in and out of the harbor, that no one would allow a group of Frenchmen to come in and steal children. Neither the

English nor the Acadians. It was an English ship that took J-B's son. They will never allow a French one to do that."

"I don't think he'll have a problem. He will send men in. There are genuine spies in Louisbourg, you know. Men who speak perfect English. Where do you think I learned my perfect English? And how to spy?"

I must have looked at him with my thoughts on my face.

"I told you. I would never spy. And I am not spying. May I continue?"

"Were my thoughts that obvious?"

"They certainly don't tell any lies about you, Keskoua. I hope you never do anything illegal. You'll never get away with it." He moved his sweet from inside one cheek to the other. "To continue: The children are breaking the law by helping a traitor, these men will say. By sneaking food and water to LaBine and his family, they are traitors, too. That way, the English guards will unknowingly let the men from Louisbourg take them. Thinking they are from New England or Boston or somewhere that's on their side.

"But you were asking about what caused the Scotsman, Ian, to get into such terrible trouble. Weren't you? He felt he owed it to Pierre. For saving his life."

"Pierre saved this Scotsman's life?"

"Years ago. Around the time Pierre got into trouble for not signing that treaty. In fact, I think Pierre might actually have been hiding in the bush from the authorities when it happened.

"Anyway. Not every newcomer is familiar with all the animals in the bush. Ian didn't even live there. He was always here and there traveling from port to port and country to country. He has a world view, a kind heart. He was in the bush. I don't know why. Perhaps he was learning about the animals we have here. Maybe he was gathering dried up branches to keep him warm if he planned to camp outdoors for the night. I don't know and it isn't important anyway. But… He came across a bear cub."

"Oh no!"

"Oh, yes. And he not only approached it. Thinking it was lost, he picked it up."

"And mama bear came along."

"Pierre came along, too, fortunately. With a great amount of noise and yelling and jumping up and down, he was able to frighten off all three of them." Bobby laughed. "In different directions. Ooh. I shouldn't laugh. I shouldn't."

"Laughter is good for the health. But not always. Right?"

"Right." Bobby adjusted his position again. "So that is what happened to cause the Scotsman Ian to feel he owed Pierre his life. And *this* is what happened the day that condemned the Scotsman Ian to a life of avoiding the noose. Now. Let me practice being a storyteller, will you, Keskoua?"

I smiled and crossed my legs the other way.

"One day, many people watched in fear as something happened. As you know, everybody likes Pierre and some applaud him for his continuing stand. The soldiers are always there, near the dock and these 'guards,' have weapons and have been authorized to use them whenever they see a reason to do so.

"I've heard that sometimes these reasons are personal. Perhaps the reason is a woman. Perhaps the reason is nothing more than a vague dislike of a man. Oh. I am moving away from the story. Do you ever get ahead of yourself when talking about what happened?"

"Never."

"It was around this time that the children started bringing food and water to LaBine's houseboat. The adults allowed this, thinking the guards would never hurt a child. The children tried to figure out ways to get these items onto LaBine's houseboat without the guards realizing it. It was like a game to them, I guess.

"But this day, two Acadian boys—boys dressed in Mi´gmaw regalia for a reason I do not know—instead of getting into the small rowboat and going around behind LaBine's houseboat pretending to play *that* particular game, boldly stepped up to the edge of the dock. Right in front of the guards' eyes. The boys started handing things down to one of LaBine's little lads. LaBine's little lad was barely more than two or three years old. They were taking great care not to have the wee lad fall overboard.

"'Halt! Stop what you're doing there!' cried one of the guards, aiming his weapon at the boys on the dock. One of them turned and told the guard, 'Mange la merde. Eat shit.'"

"No! He didn't! Brave boy."

"That he did. And this caused the guard to cock his weapon. This is probably the only phrase the English know in French."

"Probably," I said, smiling.

"A second guard ran toward this boy to stand in front of him against his fellow soldier. Then LaBine leaped out of the houseboat onto the dock to protect the boy, too. Meanwhile, LaBine's wee lad was crying his head off in fear and this brought his mama up on deck.

"And this brought the crowd even closer. A rumble started going through the people. They were not going to stand there and allow anyone to either shoot a child or shoot a man in front of his own wife and children. Things were getting serious. Quickly.

"The first guard called out, 'Get off our land. You are an enemy of the Crown and have no right to step on our soil.' He aimed his weapon at LaBine now.

"Then Ian jumped in from… I didn't see where he came from."

"You were there?"

"I was. He threw his leg around the first guard's leg, causing the first guard to fall. And causing his weapon to fire."

"Oh, no," I said. "And the shot struck…?"

"It struck the other guard but not how you might be thinking. The shot went low. It went through the second guard's boot removing the tip of his big toe. We could see it through the hole in his boot. We knew it wasn't all that serious."

"So what was all the fuss about then? This Scotsman, this Ian, did no harm. In fact, he—"

"The harm was that everyone laughed at the guard who was hopping around on one foot and holding the injured one in both his hands. One of the Acadian men happened to have his fiddle. You might know Charles? He never goes anywhere without it."

I nodded. I knew him.

"So Charles started playing a tune in time with the guard's hops."

"Oh, no!" I'm sure the captain and crew up on deck must have heard my laughter from way down here in Bobby's cabin.

Bobby groaned and held his side.

"No! Really?"

"Stop it, Keskoua. I'm in pain here."

I covered my mouth but that didn't help keep the laughter from leaking out around the sides of my hand.

"Then…" Bobby put both hands on his side. "Oh. Oh dear. Then…" Laughing, he continued, "Someone began to call out words to une danse carrée, a square dance."

I doubled over.

"Stop laughing. You're making me laugh. Oh. Ow. By this time, several more guards had arrived and they snatched up Ian, placed him under arrest, and took him to a holding room."

"Under arrest for what?"

"Some balderdash about interfering with due process of law. They needed some excuse. Rage knows no bounds when a guard doing his duty is made fun of in front of those his country has conquered. And those he himself has supposed control over. The guard who did the shooting, of course had to cover his error and blame someone else. He claimed that Ian had wrested the weapon away from him and had shot his comrade himself. This to avoid the firing squad for both guards."

"Would they really put them in front of a firing squad? It wasn't the guard's fault, either. It was an accident."

"They would have, yes."

"It's very complicated, isn't it?"

"Complicated indeed. And they took the two boys away as well."

"Oh, no." My laughter disappeared like a mulumgwej, a groundhog into its hole.

"That night, Gracie and Bart Little happened to come along. If you know what I'm saying? They'd been there the entire time but had stayed out of sight. They always do when they're in Mirligueche. Among the three of us and, I must add, several others from the area, we managed to get Ian away and onto a ship."

"They didn't have guards on him?"

"One of the young women volunteered to approach the guard with naughty suggestions. She managed to take him outside and distract him long enough for us to get Ian free."

"This young woman was a…?"

"A prostitute? Not at all. She told us, 'On pain of death. Yours! Give a signal the moment he is free!' And we did. And she was safe, sound and untouched.

"We got him to a ship. A ship with a neutral owner, captain and crew. By coincidence, this one."

I had been on this ship before. I knew the captain. I knew him well. Although I had not known him when he was called Captain Rich, I knew him well enough to know that he no longer wished to be known as Captain Rich, former pirate, but only as Captain Richard, or better yet, only as "Captain," without a name attached at all. So Agada had not completely lied to me about her Ian having arrived on a pirate ship. Ian had arrived on a "pirate's ship." That made me smile.

"Hence, Ian ended up in a wikuom in the bush near the village of Matuwes."

"You didn't go with them?"

"I returned to Louisbourg immediately. When something like that happens, every guard looks upon every face with renewed suspicion. I returned as immediately as I could, that is. There are not many means of transportation from Mirligueche to Louisbourg, or back again, as you might imagine."

"What about the two young boys?"

Bobby shook his head.

"Nothing?"

"Nothing."

"How did J-B react to this?"

"Not well. Not well at all. I'm surprised there wasn't smoke coming out of his ears. I'm afraid he's going to do something crazy. Really crazy. This was months ago and if you add on the promise of the English, with the signing of that 'peace' treaty two months ago and with nothing coming of it…"

I would wait until we arrived in Mirligueche to put my mind and heart toward helping out with this problem. There was nothing I could do now, from here, except tend to the wounded young man in my care.

"Another sweet? Your time is up."

"Already? But you said—"

"I lied. I can do it, too, when I need to." I got up off the floor. "Time to change your wrappings. And I think you should find yourself a new jacket." I helped him remove it. "This one is covered in dried blood. That's not good. It will draw microbes. Not to mention attention. It looks terrible." I held his jacket out for him to see.

The corners of his mouth turned down. "I like that jacket. A lot."

"Here." I handed him the sweet and his second little bottle of laudanum. "Before you take this, go ask one of the crew if he has something that might fit you. You need to cover up your wound before we get to Mirligueche. We don't want anybody asking questions, do we?"

He shook his head.

"I'm going up on deck. Do what I told you. Then sleep." At the door, I paused. "You are an excellent storyteller, Bobby. I'll teach you everything I can. Whatever you want to know."

"Thank you. I lied, too. I really did want to meet you even though I already knew you. And learn how to be a storyteller. I had a dream."

Thirteen

I had no sooner got up onto the deck when I heard the captain curse.

"Christ a-mighty. There's fooking flags for Tebouque."

Tebouque? I was about to ask the captain where this place was but realized he meant Chebogue. Our words were as often mispronounced by our Acadian friends as they were by the Maudits anglaises and others from everywhere else.

"We have to fooking stop near fooking Tebouque again." He grabbed a telescope near the wheel and held it up to his eye. "And it looks like a fooking female, too. A young one though. And dressed like a fooking New Englander. All's we need is one of them bastards on my ship to give it more bad luck." He turned to me. "Sorry, ma'am. We've been diverted."

He shouted unintelligible commands to his crew then called out to Sofia, who was standing by the rail near the bow. "You might consider taking your granny down to the galley. The language might be getting a bit rough for her. Some of my crew have no fooking respect for the elderly."

At this, Sofia threw an amused glance at me and her mouth said, *Granny?* She stepped toward me and took my elbow. "Come on, you poor old dear. Let's get you back down and see if we can find this 'galley' he's talking about. Watch your step now."

"Stop it," I laughed as I shrugged her off. "I know where the galley is. I'll lead the way."

I heard a splash and assumed the anchor had been dropped.

"Looks like their boat is already in the water, Cap'n. And it looks like a few pigeons along with your 'pigeon' will be coming on board. There's pigeon cages and I see movement in them."

Another voice said, "Looks like they's fast rowers. Good. We won't be delayed too long."

I turned back toward the captain. "The galley? Really. You're sending us to your kitchen? Not to our cabins?"

"The galley. My kitchen. Yes. Have some tea. Have water. Have whiskey. Have something. Only stay there until I give an order otherwise!"

"Yes, sir. No problem, sir. Whatever you desire, sir."

Sofia whispered, "I don't think you should be saying it like *that* to the captain!"

"Did he flinch?"

"No."

"Did he throw me in irons?"

"No."

"Is she trying to be funny?"

"That's just her, sir. Captain sir. You'll get used to it."

"I hope so. For her sake," said Captain. But he said this with a smile tugging at one side of his face. "Or else she'll be going overboard."

Sofia's gasp made me laugh again. "Don't worry, Sofia. I've avoided that particular death before. But I know someone who didn't." I took her arm and led her toward the doorway below the helm. "The galley will be this way."

"How do you know so much about ships?"

"It's a long story. Shall I tell it to you? It's about a woman we called Vaca Imunda. It means filthy cow. She went overboard. A shark got her."

"Is it a true story?"

"It is."

"I don't want to hear about it then. And I don't want you to annoy Captain again. I don't want him throwing you into the water." She followed me down the ladder.

"I don't want him to do that either. But I doubt he will. I'm a paying passenger, aren't I?"

At the bottom of the ladder, she turned to face me, the worry still on her face.

"It's na to´q. He knows me. I've traveled with him many times. He's just trying to get you going."

***

I heard Captain's voice coming from above. "I welcome you aboard, young lady. The other passengers are below. In the galley."

"Thank you for stopping, Captain. I want to go to my cabin. With my things."

"Those pigeons are yours, too?"

"Of course not. I don't want those filthy creatures anywhere near me."

"Very well," came Captain's voice. He then muttered something to, I imagined, a crew member.

I heard the word "baggage" and a returning mutter, and after much clunking and banging, a crew member appeared at the bottom of the ladder with a suitcase in each hand. These, he set on the floor, then reached up for another that was being handed down to him.

The young lady's voice: "Step back. I don't want you looking up my skirt."

"Yes, ma'am. Er, I mean, no ma'am."

I saw a shadow as a crew member, already below, took away two of the suitcases. The shadow returned to collect the third suitcase, then left.

"Where did you go?" demanded the young lady, now standing in full view of Sofia and me through the doorway of the galley. She looked over at us. "What are you staring at?"

Sofia suddenly found something interesting at the bottom of her teacup. I continued to stare.

The young lady was about seveneen years old, fairly tall, slim, exceptionally pretty, with yellow hair peeking out from under her bonnet. She was dressed as a New Englander, much as Sofia was, but also like Sofia, there was something very un-New-Englander about her.

To see if I could learn something more, I spoke in French. "Bonjour. Je m'appelle Keskoua, et c'est Sofia. Vous êtes?"

The young lady did not respond.

"How about English, then? Good day. I am Keskoua. This is Sofia. You are?"

Still no response.

"Maybe she's deaf," suggested Sofia, now looking at the young lady. "And can only read lips. That's too bad. She's really pretty."

"She's not deaf at all," came Captain's voice from the ladder. "Any more tea left?" He stepped around the young lady to come through the doorway. "I'm sorry I had to put you ladies here. It's just that… Well. The last time we were asked to stop near Tebouque, it was a ruse."

"A ruse?" Sofia asked.

He lifted the lid off the teapot and looked inside. "It means deception or trick. Ah, good. There's some left." He stepped over to the cupboard and removed a cup from one of the shelves. He filled his cup.

"I know what it means. I just want to know what happened. Uh, Captain. Sir."

"Someone came aboard armed with a weapon and searching for one of my crew."

"Oh, dear. That must have been terribly frightening. Was he an enemy soldier or something?"

"No. *She* was a jealous and very angry wife."

I covered my laugh with both hands.

"What are you doing standing out there like a lost soul?" he said to the young lady. "Get in here. Have some tea. Ladies? This is Élisabeth. But she prefers Eliza. And Eliza, this is Keskoua, and this is Sofia." He stepped back toward the ladder then glanced down the passageway. "Ah. Our young man is awake. Barely."

I heard a mumbled greeting from Bobby.

"The head's that way." Captain pointed toward it with an elbow. "And tea is right here. And company. Female company."

Looking groggy, Bobby appeared at the doorway.

Bobby looked absolutely nothing like he had. He was dressed like a New England gentleman. His hair was pulled back into a knot at the base of his skull. He had frills at his wrist and he even had boots on. I would not have recognized him. But I did. I had seen him before. In Mirligueche. Dressed like this.

Bobby's mouth opened in an extra wide smile. He raised his hands to shoulder level—one of them not as high as the other—and turned around to let us see his entire outfit.

"Recognize me now, Keskoua?"

I did and was embarrassed beyond embarrassment to admit it to myself. Had I not recently thought poorly of the unnamed man on our boat trip to Chief Jumping Robin's village for not seeing the person behind the clothing?

"You do look somewhat familiar," I said.

Captain wrapped one of his big hands around the top rung of the ladder and as he worked his way up it, he said, "I'll expect all of you in my quarters this evening at eight bells."

"Eight bells?" asked Sofia.

"It's a measurement of time," I said.

Captain's voice came down the ladder. "For what I believe will be a sumptuous dinner. Cook's on break right now. He's sleeping." I heard Captain's footsteps walk away then return. "He's the one with the jealous, angry wife. He is still recovering from the gunshot."

"Oh. Is there anything I can do?"

"Best not, ma'am. It was the healer in Tebouque got him in trouble in the first place."

This time, Sofia was the one who laughed.

***

Bobby worked his way into the galley where he lowered himself carefully onto the chair across from the young lady.

Sofia pulled a cup off the counter and poured tea for him. "Sugar?"

"Please."

She added sugar, stirred it and put it in front of him.

He raised the cup to his mouth and took a small sip. He set the cup down and smiled at the young lady. Or maybe it wasn't a smile. I think the word for it is "smirk."

"Have you met my friends, here? Ah. Of course, you have. I heard Captain introducing you to them and them to you. But I didn't hear you say hello. And you have this young woman here…" He indicated Sofia. "… thinking you are deaf so is no doubt concerned about your welfare. Is that how you repay such kindness?"

I leaned over toward Sofia and quietly said, "I don't think it's the medicine I gave him. I think they know each other?"

"Oh, yes. We know each other all right," said Bobby without taking his eyes off the young lady's. "So, Sweet-Corn. You've changed your mind?"

Fourteen

I don't know about Sweet-Corn's mind, but my mind was still running around inside my head like a bee inside a bearberry flower as we made our way into the captain's quarters that evening. Bobby and this young lady knew each other. And it appeared they didn't much like each other. She still hadn't said a word to any of us. I didn't know whether we should call her Eliza, which Captain had said her name was, or Sweet-Corn, which Bobby had called her and which I doubted the Grandfathers had given her even though it sounded like one of our names for one of our people. Or Élisabeth. The way Captain has said it made it sound French. Could she be Acadian? More likely Métis by her facial structure.

I had checked Bobby's wound again and was pleased that everything about it was na to´q. There was no redness anywhere around it, much to my relief. And to Bobby's relief, too, he said. I put salve on it and applied new cloth. The used cloth I gave to Cook to burn. While I was with Bobby, I knew he knew I was ready to burst out of my bearberry flower if he didn't tell me more about Sweet-Corn, but he had said nothing, and I hadn't asked.

***

The captain's quarters were not as I remembered them. They now had pink walls and lace and frills everywhere and amazing furniture. On the dining table were plates and glasses and bowls and utensils. It was covered with what looked like silk so I couldn't see what the actual table looked like, but its legs matched the chairs. The purple chairs. Chairs that glowed enough to have been made in Montréal and covered with beeswax like our armoire had been.

Captain was standing at the head of the table, smiling. Through the porthole behind him, I could see calm waters and not too distant hills slowly moving past us. Or, I suppose, we were moving past them. That was the strangest thing about being inside a ship. It was like things were passing *us*. In a canoe, we always knew exactly where we were going.

"Your chairs and table are beautiful, Captain. They're new. To me, at least. Where were they made?"

"Here and there."

I see. "The color is very different from what I've ever seen. Not that I've seen a lot. But purple? And how can they be painted without covering over the grain of the wood?"

"Please be seated," he said. "No, no. Here." I knew this was the place of honor at a dining table, at the host's right hand.

To Bobby, who was at my elbow, Captain said, "And you, young man, will sit to the left of me. This young lady…"

"Sofia," she said.

"Sofia." He nodded. "Sofia may sit beside either Keskoua or Bobby. Élisabeth—uh, sorry, Eliza—can decide for herself when she gets here. *If* she gets here."

Sofia came around the table to stand beside me. "I think you are mistaken about her, Captain, Sir. She *must* be deaf. Who could not have heard those bells ringing on and on like that?"

"You can trust the captain," said Bobby. "The last thing that girl is, is deaf."

The Captain sat and moved his hands around telling us we should sit now, too.

"How do you know her?" I asked as I pulled my chair in.

Bobby said, "We trained together." His eyes met mine full on. "In that special school I was telling you about. Remember? That *private* school?"

"And you, Captain? How do you know her?"

"The wood is not painted. Nor is it stained. That's its natural color. It comes from the West Indies." There was that partial smile again. "Or so I've been told."

I see.

"Aha. She has deigned to honor us with her presence," the Captain said, bobbing up from his chair, then just as quickly settling back down. "Will you join us?" This he said without hand motions.

The young lady, now dressed in a similar manner to Bobby, stood outside the entranceway. Her yellow hair was tied at the back of her neck like Bobby's was; she wore trousers and a vest and a jacket with frills at the cuffs.

Without looking at anyone, she entered the cabin and sat beside Sofia.

To me, Sofia said, "She's two-spirited." To Eliza, she said, "You're two-spirited?"

In a deepened voice, the young lady said, "What, pray tell, does that phrase mean?"

Before Sofia could speak, Bobby laughed and said, "That, she is not. Trust me."

This caused the young woman's eyes to shoot arrows at Bobby's.

For an uncomfortable moment, all I could hear was the clock ticking behind me on the wall of the captain's quarters.

"So," I said, bending around to look at her. "I understand you went to school with Bobby here."

Her next flash of rage at Bobby told me this was true. The "special school," the spy school, and the learning of other languages to perfection would also be true.

"She excelled at everything they threw at her," Bobby said. "Isn't that right, Sweet-Corn?"

She made no comment but I saw her chest rise and fall and her face relax when a man I assumed was Cook appeared at the door with a tray full of covered dishes.

"Ah. Look who's here," said Captain. "What delights do you have for us this evening, Cook?"

Cook placed the tray at the end of the table and with a grand flourish, lifted one of the covers off. "We begin with an appetizer of coq au vin but with partridge in lieu of fowl." Here, limping slightly, he brought one bowl around to the captain and set it in front of him. He returned to the end of the table to collect the other four bowls and present them, first to me, then to Bobby, to Sofia, and lastly, to the young lady.

Cook filled our glasses: wine glasses with wine and water glasses with water. He set a teapot on the table and alongside it, he placed four sets of teacups and saucers. "In case you prefer tea." He limped away.

Sofia reached immediately for a teacup and saucer for me and then for her. She filled our cups.

Bobby raised his water glass. "To the continuation of our safe voyage."

Sofia and I raised our teacups.

An elderly man skitted in with what I guessed was a sugar bowl. He placed this in front of Sofia, along with a small spoon, then disappeared like smoke into the passageway.

"Thanks to Captain," I said. And more loudly and toward the door, "And to Cook. And to his… What do you call Cook's helpers?"

Captain set his wine glass back on the table and picked up his fork. "That depends. Enjoy." He dipped into his bowl. "Eat. Eat."

***

The meal was excellent. The conversation that followed it ranged from amusing to shocking to worry inducing.

Sweet-Corn, young Eliza, was on her way to Mirligueche and from there to Louisbourg then to Boston to study more about law. It was not possible for her to become a lawyer. She was female. The best she could hope for was court reporter. And even then, it would be difficult for a female with no local connections to get a position doing that. So she would pose as a male. She would go by the name of Lester. And, tonight, she was practicing. She asked for our cooperation and we agreed, Sofia with giggles.

"Lester" had gone to Chebogue to spend time with a man who knew special codes for writing down spoken words quickly. In several languages. But this would be a secret. As far as anyone in Boston or anywhere else would know, Eliza-Lester could take notes only in English. But she would, when overhearing those who were speaking French, Dutch, Portuguese, Italian and even Mi´gmaq, scribble the codes and send them by pigeon to the man in Chebogue. He, in turn, would get these messages to Louisbourg from where they would go to France.

And no, she didn't like pigeons. "I feel as though they're looking at me all the time. Judging me. I hate them. Dirty, filthy things. All they do is coo and poo."

"And save lives," I said.

At this, she shrugged and turned away from me.

"I want to go to Boston, too," said Sofia. "What's it like there? Have you been there yet?"

"Not yet. I'm to be met at the Boston Harbor docks by a man named Edward. An old man. I hope he is still alive by the time I get there." She laughed but without humor.

"Edward? Edward Gooden by chance?" I asked.

"Do you know him?"

What could I say to that? "I've heard of him."

Sofia coughed.

Bobby changed positions in his chair.

Captain leaned forward to put his elbows onto the table. "There's no need to lie, Keskoua. My cabin is soundproofed. And idiot-proofed as well, I hope." Here, his eyes shot back and forth from Bobby's to

Eliza-Lester's, then to Sofia's. "My dear wife did the decorating on my orders, much to her dismay. Behind the walls… I think if you examine them more closely, Keskoua, you'll realize they are much thicker than they were. They have been soundproofed. These fooking frillies and pink things are merely a disguise, a distraction. They're disgusting but necessary. I still wake up in the middle of the night thinking I've died and been sent to some brothel-house hell as an eternal punishment for past sins. My wife made me promise never to tell anyone she was the decorator of this fluffy sanctuary. But here I am telling you, am I not?"

"An excellent diversion," I said. "We did the same with our inn at Annapolis Royal. We made it look like a place for spies to congregate to take the attention away from its owner."

"Do you know him?" asked Eliza-Lester.

"It's owner? Of course I do. He's my husband."

"I mean Edward."

"I do. He's trustable. But he is now a widower again so not trustable in all matters. Do you understand what I'm saying?"

Eliza-Lester glanced over at Bobby. "Oh, yes. I absolutely understand what you're saying."

Fifteen

I slept well that night in spite of my excitement about being able to see Mak again. It had been only days but it felt like moons had gone by since I'd last been with him. I was worried about what Bobby had said about J-B, too, but that would have to wait until I spoke with J-B himself. No point in worrying about something somebody heard about something that somebody else might have seen or heard. If, when I spoke with J-B and learned that his plan—whatever it was—could be dangerous, or if he even had a plan in the first place, then I would have something real to worry about. Then, if I managed to change his mind about doing a possibly dangerous thing, I wouldn't have had anything to worry about in the first place. I would wait.

Bobby, Sofia and I were alone for the morning meal in the captain's quarters. We were closing in on the port at Mirligueche so Captain was at the helm. When I asked Bobby where Eliza-Lester was, he told me she was "battening down her baggage."

"She's what?"

"We're docking. Surely, you know what happens when any ship docks at Mirligueche."

"What's he talking about?" asked Sofia.

Bobby said, "She is securing her baggage by locking it down. To prevent them from seeing anything she might need for her future position in Boston. And possibly taking it."

"They? Who's they?"

"The people at Mirligueche," I told her. "They live by the old ways of our people."

"What does that have to do with locking up her stuff? Or, his stuff, I guess I have to say now?"

"Do you want to explain this, Bobby?"

"I get to play storyteller again?" He turned to Sofia. "Nobody owns the land."

"Of course not."

"Everyone shares."

"Why would they not? If you need something and I have it... Oh." Sofia's face brightened.

"That's right," said Bobby. "When a ship docks, it needs to restock with food and water. Some of these things are available without question or coin at Mirligueche. The men there hunt and fish and the women also have objects a ship's crew might need or want. They give them to the sailors. This was always our way but things have changed and most of us have adapted to the ways of the newcomers. Those of us who live near busier ports have learned the ways of those who own these ships. Those who live near Mirligueche have not been so lucky."

"What are you saying?"

"What I'm saying is, the men at Mirligueche have been boarding the ships that dock there and taking whatever they need."

"Oh."

"That's right. And those who anchor near the port of Mirligueche are not pleased with this. They do not understand the old ways. Or perhaps I should say, they do not *agree* with the old ways."

From the top deck, Captain's voice boomed down to us. "Get ready to be invaded, passengers! They don't speak much in the way of French or English, but there's no need to be afraid. They're good, kind lads, just taking what their families need."

Eliza-Lester's face appeared at the doorway. "Come with me," she said. "My cabin locks."

We were no sooner inside Eliza-Lester's cabin when we heard voices. Excited voices. Voices in my Mi´gmaw language but with a very slight difference in the way they said some of the words.

"Look at this," said the first voice. "It's a knife. A beautiful one."

"Watch where you're swinging that thing, Young Dove Man."

The first voice, Young Dove Man, said, "Hey. May I test its sharpness on your braid?"

Laughter, then, "Get away with that."

Another voice, most likely an older man said, "Look what I found over here. Nice."

Young Dove Man's companion said, "Is that blood?"

Young Dove Man said, "Is that a hole in it?"

The deep voice replied with, "Probably shot."

At this, Bobby turned to me and whispered, "They've got my jacket."

"Don't put it back," came the voice of Young Dove Man's companion. "My mother knows how to get blood out of things. I'll take it."

"What about the hole?" asked Young Dove Man.

"She'll fix that, too."

A fourth voice said, "Beads. Boxes of them. Who wants these?"

Young Dove Man's companion said, "Giju´ will welcome a blood-stained jacket with a hole in it, but she has told me, if I ever bring home any more beads, she'll shove them up my ass."

Laughter.

"Let's go," said the man with the deep voice. "We take only what we need."

Mutterings of agreement preceded the shuffling of feet and low voices.

After a moment or so, Captain called down. "All's clear. You can come up now."

Sixteen

Waiting at the foot of the gangplank was a frantic Marguerite.

"Keskoua. Keskoua. Merci à Dieu que vous êtes ici! Thank God, you're here. We need you. We need you."

When she grabbed my arm, my munti almost fell off my opposite shoulder.

"What's going on?"

"The wife of Pierre. The baby. It's coming."

I called back to Bobby and Eliza-Lester, "Take Sofia to the inn. Then go find J-B and have him meet you there."

Eliza-Lester pointed a finger at her chest as she made an impatient face at me.

"No. Not you. You keep an eye on Sofia. And all of you, tell J-B and Mak exactly everything you told me."

Bobby bowed his head at me and started off. Eliza-Lester saluted with her wrong hand. Sofia looked around like she'd just woken from a deep sleep and said, "What's going on?"

Marguerite yanked me once again and dragged me along with her at a speed I was surprised she could manage.

I asked, "Where's Tugwiet? Shouldn't she be looking after Maggie Deux?"

"Maggie Deux? Who's this 'Maggie Deux?' Ridiculous. Why do you call her that? Her name is Marguerite. The same as mine."

"That's exactly why we have to have special names for most of you. I swear, every woman who is not called Marie is called Marguerite! And every second Acadian man is a Jean-Baptiste."

"Maybe I should become Pope and declare a law. I'm sorry, but there are only so many French saints to name our children after. Oh, Keskoua. There's bad news regarding Tugwiet. I think it was only a matter of time, but..." Here, we had reached the edge of the dock and the rail of Pierre's houseboat. She leaned close to my ear to whisper, "The granddaughter of Tugwiet has been taken."

My gasp brought the guard closer to us. "What's wrong with you? Do you have a disease? No one with a disease may come near our people."

"Mon Dieu, espèce d'idiot," Marguerite spat at him. "Occupe-toi de tes affaires. Mind your own business."

The guard huffed and took a step back. I think out of fear of Marguerite, not of any imagined disease I might have been harboring.

Marguerite changed to English. "This woman is a highly respected healer from Annapolis Royal. She is here because of you and your ilk."

That wasn't true but I didn't correct her and I think I was able to keep my face from saying anything to the guard.

"If it were not for you, we would still have *our* healer here instead of off searching for her granddaughter that YOU have allowed to be taken by THEM."

"I, uh... I—"

"Don't you *dare* say you know nothing of this. You know everything of this. This taking of our children to sell as slaves."

Another guard had approached and I could see two more rushing toward us. Behind me, I could hear footsteps.

"Marguerite..." I said.

"You stay out of this. I'm talking to these people. These guards. Whom are they guarding exactly?"

"We guard everyone," said our guard. "Everyone. Even the Indians and half-breeds. And there is no slavery for anyone to be sold into around here. You need to get with the times, madam."

"I think you need to get with the times, sir. They are taking our children away to be sold as slaves."

The guard who was now standing behind my right shoulder, near my munti, spoke. "Slavery is discouraged where I come from."

"And where is that? The moon?"

"I, uh." This guard was silenced as well by Marguerite's rage.

"Slavery is discouraged by many of those who live in Massachusetts," said our guard. "Any ships taking these Indians away have to pass by Boston Harbor to replenish supplies. They'll be noticed. If they are spotted, their names could be blackened, their businesses destroyed depending on who sees them. I know of no one who would wish to take that chance. They could not get away with it."

"Not for long, at least," said one of the guards behind our guard.

"So you say. Slavery is still allowed, *discouraged* or not. Come here, Keskoua. Let me help you into the boat."

"Hey, hey," said the guard behind me. "No one is allowed on board that houseboat. Or off it, either."

By now, I could see a worried Pierre, called LaBine now according to Bobby, standing at the opening that led below decks.

Our guard said, "Indians don't count." Then to me, he said, "You signed that treaty? The one in June? The one promising peace on both sides?"

I dug around in my munti and brought out a paper, the treaty that bore my signature. I showed it to the guard behind me before showing it to our guard. Peace on both sides? No. Peace still went one way only. From our side to theirs.

The guard behind me asked our guard, "What's it say, Timmy? Is she telling the truth?"

"She is."

"But you," and here, Timmy pointed his musket at Marguerite, "are not allowed. Step back. Horace? Help the Indian down."

The man behind me stepped closer to take my elbow and with surprising gentleness and respect, he helped me down into the houseboat of Pierre and Maggie Deux LaBine.

Seventeen

The guards had not allowed Marguerite on the houseboat itself, but they had allowed her to sit on the dock beside it. They had even brought a chair for her. Although I was below decks, we could still hear each other.

Maggie Deux was doing well with her labor, but I can't say the same for her husband. I think it was the first time Pierre had been delegated as assistant midwife. I don't think he liked it. His face would get very red then very pale. When it got pale, he would ask to be excused. When this happened, I knew he was up on deck emptying his stomach over the rail. I could hear gentle splashing and I could also hear Marguerite's laughter.

"Marguerite! It's not nice to make fun of your children."

"I know."

This made me laugh and it made Maggie Deux laugh as well. This helped with her labor. Her child would be a happy one despite the circumstances of its birthplace.

The baby came out just as Pierre arrived back in the room.

"It's a boy," I said, as I placed it on Maggie Deux's chest. She put her arms around him. "Hand me those cloths, Pierre."

Pierre did. "A boy, you say? A boy? Wonderful. Thank you, my dear wife. Thank you. What shall we name him?"

"Charles, I think. What about Charles?"

"Charles it is. Sorry I was acting like such a baby myself. Getting sick and all. It's only because I love you and couldn't bear seeing you in such pain."

I wiped the baby off, wrapped it in a cloth, and handed it to Pierre. His eyes, reddened and wet from vomiting, looked at his new son with tenderness. "Good day, my son. Welcome to the world."

The baby made a sound and Pierre's eyes widened. "Oh, am I hurting it?"

"No, you aren't. Give him to me. He wants his mama." I handed the boy back to Maggie Deux and called out to Marguerite. "You're a grandmother again. It's a boy."

"Wonderful news! Wonderful! Is everyone all right? Including my son?"

"Everything is well, Marguerite." By now, I could hear voices from above as women and men alike began to congratulate Marguerite on the birth of her latest grandson.

"I had nothing to do with it," I heard her laugh as she tried to pretend she wasn't proud of her son and his wife. "Nothing at all."

Eighteen

"*Mpenzi*, my love." Mak's arms were around me and his lips were on mine the moment I stepped inside the inn.

From somewhere over in a corner I heard Sofia's voice, "For the love of God, you two, there are people in here, you know."

I pulled myself away from Mak. Even at our age, he could still take my breath away. "Greetings, oqoti. I trust you are well after our lengthy separation."

Mak laughed. "Two days equals two years for me as well when we are apart, my love."

"Do they always talk to each other like that?" asked the voice of Eliza-Lester.

Sofia answered, "Mama told me she reads a lot of books from New England. I guess Mak does, too."

"Maybe I'm not as excited about going to New England after all, if they talk like that."

By this time, Mak was guiding me toward a large table under a window near the front of the inn where Eliza-Lester and Bobby sat with bowls of food and cups and half-full glasses in front of them. Bobby was grinning ear-to-ear. Eliza-Lester, a spoon in her fist, was scooping food out of her bowl.

Sofia, holding a jug and with a cloth hanging off the opposite arm was standing behind them. Her eyes were pointed toward the ceiling.

"Are you hungry, *mpenzi*?" Mak let go of me to pull out a chair at the table.

"I am." I sat as he guided the chair inward. "Thank you, my darling husband."

We kissed again.

"You two are disgusting."

Bobby laughed. "You work here now, 'Miss Sofia.' I don't think you're allowed to have opinions of the patrons."

Eliza-Lester giggled. "But when I get my law certificate, I'll certainly defend you against any charges for that." She dipped her spoon into her bowl. "For a fee, of course."

"She's allowed to have opinions of the patrons," said Mak. "She is not allowed to voice those opinions. And she is especially not allowed to show them with her actions. Especially her *facial expressions*?"

"You hired her?" I asked him. "She's been here for… How long? Perhaps two hours?"

"Could I say no?"

"I hope I have such good luck getting a placement in Boston," said Eliza-Lester, pushing away her bowl with a thumb. "That was good."

An angry shout drew my attention to the other side of the inn. The long bar that our friends in Annapolis Royal had made for us, ran almost from wall to wall. A flat panel at each end stretched out to touch each wall. From where I sat, I could see the hinges underneath these panels that would allow them to be lifted to get in and out from behind it, where the glowing armoire sat, the armoire that Mak had been so protective of when it was being loaded onto the ship that would bring it from there to here. It held wine glasses and beer mugs, some of the mugs with writing on them. I could see no bottles of spirits, though, like those that filled the many shelves at our Messenger Pigeon Inn back home.

Toward the far end of the bar was a table surrounded by men, most of them looking mixed, but all of them dressed like my people.

Mak leaned over to whisper into Sofia's ear loudly enough for the rest of us to hear: "Voicing or showing one's opinion in a public house, if it differs from that of another—no matter what that opinion is—can be dangerous. See?"

I recognized one of the men. The one who was now rising from his chair and reaching around to his right hip where a knife sat in its leather sheath. It was a brother-in-law of J-B. "I'll have none of that," he said in a mixture of French and Mi´gmaq. "We are going. And we are going tomorrow. Those bastards will release my brother…" He pulled out his knife and pierced the air above him with it. "… or someone will DIE! I'm sick of waiting and waiting and waiting while they promise and promise and promise but do NOTHING."

"Uncle. Uncle James. Take it easy," said a voice I recognized from earlier, from the ship we had come in on. It was one of the younger ones who had come aboard searching for things they needed. He, too, spoke in a combination of French and Mi´gmaq.

"Is that J-B's son?" I whispered. "He grew since the last time I saw him."

"It is," said Bobby. "He's called Jeune Jean. Young Jean instead of Jean le Jeune, Jean Junior. He won't tell anyone his Spirit Name."

"Why? What is it?" asked Sofia.

"If I told you, he'd probably stick a knife into my throat." Making a scary face at Sofia, he leaned forward. "Maybe even into yours!"

"That bad?" I asked.

"Worse than yours," Bobby said, laughing. "If that's even possible."

"You told me your name means Breaking of the Dawn," said Mak, pretending to frown at me as if he didn't know. "Have you been keeping secrets from me?"

"Don't feel singled out, Mak." Bobby put his spoon into his bowl and pushed it away. "That was good."

"He's right, James. Sit." This came from a young man about the same age as Jeune Jean. It would be the one they had called Young Dove Man. I recognized the voice. "We'll plan something else. Don't worry."

The angry James replaced the knife into its sheath, and he sat.

"What's going on over there?" I asked Bobby.

There were seven of them. There was no food on their table. No teapots or mugs or glasses. Merely condiments and settings of spoons, knives and napkins, most of which had been pushed aside to make room for elbows.

"What are they arguing about?"

"Just listen. But don't let them catch on that you're listening." Bobby pulled his empty bowl back and leaned over it. He spoke loudly. "Mmm. This is good, is it not, my friend Lester?"

"Oh stop it," laughed Eliza-Lester.

"I need a drink!" James banged his fist on the table. "Where's our server? I want rum."

Mak patted my shoulder then stepped away toward them.

At their table, Mak spoke in French. "Good sir. We serve only wine and only when meals are ordered."

Young Dove Man spoke. "Why don't we order some of that stew those people are eating? Sounds like they like it."

"Why would I want to eat that English swill?"

"It's actually not English swill," said one of the other men. Another of J-B's brothers-in-law, a man by the name of Philippe. "It's venison. It's good. We've had it here before when J-B was setting things up. When we were helping him. Remember? It's our own sister's recipe. Their cook even gives her the credit for it. Says he doesn't change a thing about it when he makes it."

James spoke. "Where the hell did he go anyway?"

"Who? J-B? Don't you remember?"

"Remember what?"

"J-B offered a less-illegal solution to getting back our brother and his son."

"And you disagreed with him."

Jeune Jean added, "Then Papa disagreed with you about disagreeing with him."

Bobby leaned toward me. "As you might have guessed, James is extremely distraught about François and young Paul being taken away. He's at his wits' end. His rage hasn't diminished a single degree since it happened. I think it increases at each anniversary." Bobby, face full of sadness, shook his head. "He still insists they're in prison in Boston. He prefers that over thoughts of… His mind won't accept that they could have been taken as… as slaves. He's… He's…"

"Worry can drive a person mad. So can rum. Combine the two…"

A crash at the table where the men were, drew my eye again. James was standing. His chair was on the floor behind him. He was shaking his fist at Young Dove Man.

Mak called out, pointing to the back corner doorway at our side of the inn. "Sofia. This will be your second effort at serving a meal. Go to the kitchen and bring out…" He turned to the men. "How many bowls of venison stew, gentlemen?"

Mutters went around the table as the men nodded to each other.

"Looks like it will be seven bowls," said Jeune Jean. "We get wine with that?"

"It comes with wine, yes, young man. But what is that in your pocket there?"

"What?" said James. "You little thief. You're the one who took my bottle of rum." James started to move around the table to get closer to Jeune Jean, but he was stopped by Philippe.

"Let him have it. It wasn't yours to begin with. They gave it to *him*. Remember?"

"Who gave that young boy rum?" I whispered.

Bobby said, "That's another big problem these days. Whenever our people go on their ships to look for something in exchange for the food, water and other supplies we provide to them, they give them rum instead."

"No."

"Yes."

Nineteen

Carrying a huge tray in front of her, with from what I could see were four full bowls, Sofia slowly approached the men's table. I was surprised she wasn't spilling any over the edges of the bowls.

Mak rushed to her and took the tray. "Like this," he said, swinging it around and up to shoulder level with one hand supporting it from below. "And this way, if someone comes too close to you, you can raise it over your head like this." He demonstrated.

Sofia's mouth popped open.

He set the tray on the table. "We'll practice with one bowl at a time."

A man I did not know appeared at my left side with my bowl of stew which he slid onto the table in front of me.

"Wela´lin. Uh, Merci. Thank you."

"De rien, Madame Keskoua." Hands behind his back, he bowed slightly then disappeared into the kitchen.

Over at the men's table, Sofia was adjusting small bowls of salt and pepper to put them in reach of the patrons.

Heading to the kitchen, Mak called out. "*Three more. One on a tray.*"

"Where's mine?" demanded James.

"Here," said Jeune Jean, sliding his bowl across the table to James. "She probably heard you say you didn't want any." He closed one eye at Sofia. "I'll wait for this lovely lady to bring mine especially to me. And I might have seconds. Perhaps even thirds if I know she will be the one serving it."

Sofia picked up the tray and quickly moved off into the kitchen with it. From where I sat, I could see her flushed face. She would have to get used to men saying such things to her.

"I still say my way is the way it has to be done," said James. "We've tried everything else, haven't we?"

Jeune Jean replied, "But like Papa says, we can't do it. We've signed the peace agreement. We will not break our word."

"There is no peace. That agreement was supposed to be for both sides. Not just us agreeing from our side."

"It was for both sides," said Philippe. "Both sides signed it."

"And you trust them," James snapped at him. "Did you read it? Did it say that? Did it say the English promise that our young children can fish without breaking the law?"

"That's what it said."

"And how do you know that? For certain?"

Silence.

"You can no more read than I can, dear brother. How do you know they agreed? Obviously, it didn't say that, or our brother would be sitting here with us and so would our nephew, young Paul."

Silence.

"But Papa said—"

"I know what your papa said, Jeune Jean. He's a fool. We must not *pretend* to take a ship. We must take one for real. Let them know we mean business. Kill, if necessary."

My gasp must have been loud as three of the men turned toward our table. I quickly looked down at my stew. "You're right, Bobby. It is delicious."

Then Sofia was diverting their attention from my gasp, too. She was on her way to their table, the big tray held at shoulder level with one bowl on top. Mak was behind her, a bowl in each hand. I don't know how she did it, but she kept her attention on the tray and got it to the table. She set it down.

"For you, sir," she said to Jeune Jean.

"Huzzah, Sofia," Mak cheered. "You did it." He set one bowl in front of a man I knew as Salmon and the other bowl in front of a man they called Lobster.

Lobster liked to dive underwater to hunt for them and that's where he got his name. But only some called him that. It was not his spirit name. We did not have to share what the grandfathers and grandmothers gave us as spirit names. Or, I am happy to say, in my own case, what the real meaning of our name was, to those who did not speak our language.

The men at the table, except for James, cheered.

"I overheard your conversation," Sofia said to James. "I could read it for you. I can read. Both French and English."

"Well good for you," James replied as he dipped his spoon into his bowl of stew.

"Have some respect," Jeune Jean told him.

"My apologies, young lady. Hmm. Good stew. Yes. But I do not want to know exactly what it says. If I do, then my plan will be for nothing and I will be hanged for piracy. Best I not know exactly what it says then, oui?" He took another mouthful of stew.

"You're a fool," said the man at the far end of their table. A man who, as yet, had said nothing. "I'm with J-B."

"Then you're the fool. If you were not family, I'd—"

"You'd what? What would you do to me?"

"I'd still ask you to be on my side, John Missel." He waved his spoon at Sofia, then pointed toward the far end of the table with it. "He's married to my sister. What else can I do?" Then he spoke to John Missel again. "But that's not the only reason I'd want you on my side. Being married to my sister proves you are made of iron and you have the strength of a bear." I was relieved to see that James was making jokes. He seemed to be relaxing.

"And I have the brains of a clam," replied John Missel, a big smile on his face. "It's not something I'd agree to again."

Everyone laughed.

I knew the woman they were speaking of. She was much like James: strong in her own opinion especially when protecting another. If John Missel was a bear, the sister of James was a mother bear.

"I know you don't mean that, John Missel," said Philippe through his laughter. "I think that's why you like her. She's a strong woman who keeps you out of trouble."

Everyone laughed.

"You're right, brother-in-law. And that's why I love her. She speaks her mind. I've never met a more honest person than she. I don't know what I'd do without her."

Here, Philippe reached to take hold of John Missel's hand. "Nor she, you. I know this for a fact. She has told me more than once how much she appreciates how devoted you are to her."

I could see redness crawling up from John Missel's neck.

"Come on, Philippe." Smiling with affection, he pulled his hand away from Philippe's. "Let's not spread that around, na to´q? I'm supposed to be a bear made of iron. Not a soft-hearted little boy coming home from his spirit quest."

"App? What?" said Jeune Jean and Young Dove Man at the same time.

They all laughed. Even James.

***

Mak, Bobby, Eliza-Lester and I stayed up long after the men had left. Patrons came and went. Sofia was in and out of the conversation and the kitchen as she kept our cups and glasses filled with tea and water and served the patrons. Her tray-carrying had improved greatly with all the practice she was getting. None of us consumed wine or whiskey.

Mak, of course, had been back and forth between Annapolis Royal and our new inn at Mirligueche—sometimes three times a month—to ensure it was coming along as planned. Bobby was back and forth on a regular basis between Louisbourg and Mirligueche. Eliza-Lester had only passed through Mirligueche on her way to study with the teacher in Chebogue, so was as eager as I was to hear the latest developments in Mirligueche.

Among the five of us, we had a lot of separate information. As we shared this information, our concerns grew greater and greater.

Twenty

I was awakened the next morning by a rooster's scream that was so loud, I looked around our room to see if Mak might have brought it inside as a joke. Mak was standing over me. His lips brushed my forehead. He was already dressed. "Did you sleep well, *mpenzi*?"

"I think I must be turning English. This bed is so comfortable, I don't think I can ever sleep on cedars and skins again without complaining about it."

"See? The English ways are not *all* bad."

I rolled out from under the covers. "I'm still trying to understand how they can believe in that god of theirs—who is supposed to be so loving and compassionate—yet feel superior to those whose skin is not white." I slipped out of my sleeping garment. "And use them as you would a horse or a cow. What shall I wear today? Where will I be?"

"Perhaps there are English who cannot read so don't know what that famous rabbi, Jesus, said. Only what people *said* Jesus said." He pointed at a dress in the cupboard. "You need not wear clothing for the inn today, *mpenzi*. Go visiting. Catch up with friends."

"Perhaps that's the problem, oqoti. Like James was saying. If you don't know for certain what something says, then you're not responsible for going against it." I wrapped my dress around me and tied it. "It will be so strange not having you running off on a ship every few days to come here to get things set up. Is that why you're sending me away to visit neighbors?" Laughing, I kissed his cheek. "It's going to take you a while to get used to my presence?"

"You need time to get settled in. You were right to insist that I hire J-B to help. He did a superb job. The people he hired are perfect. Especially our chef. Right from France! From a French cooking school. I don't know how he has so many connections."

"Do you know his mother, by any chance?"

Mak laughed. "That, I do."

"Speaking of hiring people…" I hung my munti over my shoulder while I pushed one foot into a moccasin. "You took a shorter time than it takes a hummingbird to beat its wings to hire Sofia." I reached down to hook my finger in the back of my moccasin to make sure it was on. I did the same with the other one.

"What? No. She told me you had hired her."

"Lovely girl, but it seems she can be as deceptive as her father was." I smiled with affection. "Remember him?"

"Who could forget Second Son? Secky. A good man at heart but perhaps too enthusiastic about… How do those New England books of yours put it? '… coming to the aid of those in peril.' Is he related to James, by any chance?"

"It's the way of our people," I said. "That's what our men do. They protect. At least, before the Newcomers came, that's what they did. It's no longer easy for them to protect anymore. There are too many things going on that cannot be protected against without…"

"We'll talk more at breakfast. I need to use the facilities." Mak placed another kiss on my forehead.

"Ah, yes. Another good thing about the English. They have 'facilities.' No one need dig a hole in the ground several times a day anymore. One big hole is all we need. And it has a seat!"

***

While I was behind the long bar, going through everything on the shelves under it and in the armoire, memorizing what was there and what we might need, the chef approached me. He wore a white jacket with black buttons and a big, puffy, white hat. His hands were behind him, not like a subservient soldier, but as though it was something he'd done since childhood. He held himself erect. Even through his jacket, I could tell he was muscled and strong.

"We've met but not officially," he said in a thick France-French accent. "I'm Georges." He made a slight bow. "Sorry, Madame Keskoua, but Mak has asked me to ask you if you wouldn't mind, please, collecting the eggs this morning."

"I think that would be fun. Of course, I will." I came out from behind the bar.

I hadn't noticed the basket he'd been holding behind his back. He moved it around in front of him but held it closely to himself, with both hands. "A dozen will be good to start with. You can access the coop by going out the front door and around behind the inn." He made no motions with his hands to direct me, or with his head either. Only his words. "Take eggs only from nests closest to the entrance. And only if they're singulars."

I frowned.

"Oh. Singulars? That means there's only one in the nest. And I say, the ones closest to the entrance because the ones at the back wall, we're leaving for them to hatch." His eyes met mine then quickly moved again to his basket. "Mostly for… for the menu. If you… If you know what I mean by that. Sorry. Madame."

I took the basket from him and both his hands went directly behind him again.

"I'm an 'Indian,'" I said. "We learn to kill our own food from the instant we leap out of our mother, tomahawk in hand. Haven't you heard?" I watched his face, waiting for him to catch the teasing in my words, but I was unable to read anything there. "The only difference is, we thank them first. Their spirit, that is. We thank their spirit for offering us their body. I'm sorry. I was trying to make light of it. I'm not squeamish about where my food comes from."

"I understood that, Madame. But you didn't have chickens and your own eggs at your other inn, did you?"

"No. Why? We had friends and family who provided those things for us. Captive chickens and cows are relatively new to my people… I… Am I missing something?"

"The chickens are fully aware of where their children will be going. Like humans—most humans, I must add—they don't like it. And another thing, try not to get too attached to any of them. Never put a name on something you're going to eat. They'll all end up in the pot eventually. One way or another. Soup or stew." He turned away on his heel, this time like a soldier, and marched away into the kitchen.

I could still remember the stories my friend Claude Guédry had told me about the way food was cooked and presented in France, to the king. I doubted that Georges, this man with the France-French accent and dressed in a white jacket with black buttons and wearing a big, fluffy, white hat, would know how to cook only soup or stew. I would no doubt enjoy some of the meals he would present to me. I would no doubt *not* enjoy others. I was willing to wait and see. It's always best to judge afterwards than before.

There was a short pause, a banging of pots and pans, then Georges called out, "Their beaks are sharp. And they use this to advantage. Oh. And be certain to close the gate immediately upon both going in and going out. Ensure that it is well-latched behind you."

I wasn't sure, but I thought I detected a stifled laugh. Not from Georges, but from Mak. Had Mak been hiding in the kitchen this entire time?

What could be difficult about collecting eggs from under tame chickens? English chickens?

I soon found out what was difficult about collecting eggs from under chickens. Not only were the chickens protective, jabbing my hand as I reached in to remove the egg from under their bellies, but the rooster, that loud screeching bird who had startled me out of a happy dream that very morning, turned out to be a fierce, protective warrior. I would name him James, despite what Chef Georges had advised. But that would be my secret name for him. I would not even share this with Mak. I didn't want Mak to know I was afraid of a bird that came barely up to my knee.

Twenty-one

Over a breakfast plate of the most delicious eggs, berries and ham I'd ever tasted, Mak, Georges and I talked about fish.

"The English own the land now," Mak said. "They own, therefore, its resources as well."

"So they claim," muttered Georges around a piece of ham. "I prefer the indigenous view of things. That nobody owns anything." He slid another piece of ham off the platter in the middle of the table onto his own plate. "But then again, I wouldn't be able to work for you, get paid, and save my money to get my wife and children over here from France, would I?"

"We need to learn how to balance," Mak said. "They're being totally selfish. They don't want anyone—even if it's a single lobster or fish to feed their own family—just taking what they want when they need it. No. They won't be making *money* selling these things then, will they? That would be bad for the *uchumi*."

"*Uchumi*?" asked Georges.

"It's Swahili. Means 'economy.'"

"Ah. The economy. Yes. To some of them, the economy is more precious than God. Especially God's laws. But wait. You speak Swahili? I mean, people in this area of the world speak many languages, but Swahili?" Georges turned to me. "Your husband is an amazing man."

"You don't need to tell me that." I bumped Mak with my shoulder."

"I am more blessed having you as my wife." He bumped me back.

"Dear Lord above," came Sofia's voice from the kitchen doorway. She was carrying a large teapot toward a table with three elderly Scottish patrons. "Can you please stop that. There's a time and a place for—"

A voice at the inn's entryway stopped Sofia from saying more. It was Jeune Jean. "There she is. I've been looking all over for you."

Sofia's face flushed as she smiled shyly at him. "Oh? Me?" She topped up the teacups for the patrons then headed for our table.

"Yes. Have you seen my friend Lewis? Young Dove Man?"

Sofia's shy smile faded. "I don't know anybody around here yet."

"We were at the table yesterday. Remember? You served us."

"That doesn't mean I know you." She topped up my tea.

"Try the Inn of the Maudits Anglaises down the road," said Georges. "He sometimes goes there."

"That's what they call it?" I asked.

"That's what I call it. I also call it the Inn of the Overcooked Duck." Georges didn't laugh but the rest of us did. Even Sofia.

"Salmon, his papa, is looking for him," said Jeune Jean. "He's all worried."

"As we all are when any of the young ones go missing lately," said Mak. "May I help with anything?"

"Tout est na´toq," said Jeune Jean, smiling at Sofia. "I'll go look around. Then I need to talk to you about something. I'll be right back."

The smile returned to Sofia's face.

***

The elderly patrons soon left, smiling and thanking Sofia, saying they had enjoyed their breakfast and would certainly return to "this lovely new inn."

Both Mak and Georges, faces beaming with well-deserved pride, returned to the kitchen and since there were no other patrons, I asked

Sofia to sit with me and have tea.

"What did you make of that conversation yesterday? Those men who were sitting over there? Were you able to hear anything? What they're planning to do?"

"Not really, but I don't know any of them, so I wasn't paying much attention to *their business*. I was trying to learn how to carry a tray, to serve patrons, not spy on anybody." The look she gave me was, I knew, intended to be scolding, but I could feel worry coming from her and I don't think the worry coming from her was just a reflection of the worry I was sending out.

"Found him. I'm back." It was Jeune Jean. Right behind him were Bobby and Eliza-Lester. "Salmon almost cried when he showed up. Young Dove Man was just relieving himself." Jeune Jean laughed as he took Sofia by the arm to help her out of her chair. "Can't even *vider nos intestins* without our parents complaining these days."

Bobby slapped Jeune Jean on the shoulder. "Thanks for finding that man for us—both of them. I knew you could do it." He tipped his head toward him and asked me, "Did you know that about this young man here? He's good at finding people. Seems to have a special gift."

"That's right," said Jeune-Jean. "That guy there…" He pointed to Eliza-Lester. "… asked me if I knew who it was got his foot shot off—"

"The foot wasn't shot off," said Eliza-Lester, sounding serious and important like I thought perhaps a real attorney would sound. "It was only his toe."

"Still… She asked me if I could find him. I said 'sure.' Then somehow, I guess because I was asking around so much, the other guy, the guy who shot that guy's… It sounds better saying he shot his foot off than just his toe."

"I know" Eliza-Lester continued. "But truth is always best in a courtroom. Thank you, Jeune Jean. Thank you for doing that and so quickly, too. You're an absolute godsend."

"A what?"

"A blessing," said Sofia.

"Don't spread it around," laughed Jeune Jean. "I'll never have time to do anything else." Here, his eyes went to Sofia. "Like being with you."

Once again, pinkness crept up Sofia's cheeks.

"So." said Bobby. "I have some great news!" He spread his arms out wide. "About Ian."

Sofia's eyebrows went together as she stepped back toward us. "Ian? My mother's Ian?"

Bobby's eyes met my questioning ones. Without turning to face Sofia, he said, "Yes. Your mother's Ian has been exonerated. Finally."

Sofia's arms went around Jeune Jean, who stood as still as an apugsign, a lynx, for the briefest of moments before his arms circled her as well. She released him almost instantly, her face turning pink again. She glanced at me.

"How can that be?" I asked.

"First thing this morning, we approached them. My burgeoning attorney friend, young Lester here, was behind it all. It was all her idea. I told her all about it last night when we—" Bobby placed one arm across Eliza-Lester's shoulders. "She wanted the chance to practice. What did we have to lose?"

"It was fun," said Eliza-Lester. "I presented Bobby as a witness. I threatened them with this and that." Here, she giggled. "I mostly wanted them to listen to our side of the story. And they did. The man who got his toe shot off is a good man."

"Never mind all that," interrupted Bobby. "The main thing is, the men admitted it had nothing to do with Ian at all. Well it did, but not the way they reported it."

"What a relief." I could feel myself relaxing as I said that. "So what are they going to do with the guards then. I hope they won't hang them. Or shoot them."

"They were warned never to lie about anything. Ever again," said Bobby. "No matter what the circumstances."

Eliza-Lester added, "The guard who was the shooter has caused problems before for the man with the missing toe. He had something on him. Information. But the secret is out now, so of no value anymore." At my frown, she continued. "Because of this secret, the shooter was able to coerce the shot man into supporting the shooter's story. That Ian had done it."

"That must have been some secret."

"It was. But the shooter holds no sway over the man with the missing toe any longer. That has been resolved." Her smile was wide and her eyes shone. Eliza-Lester was sounding confident. Practicing the defense of a client—even this one time—had made a change in her. A profound one.

"You didn't answer my question. Will anyone be hanged or shot?"

Laughing, she said, "Perhaps only the wife of the high-ranking officer that the man with the missing toe had been dallying with."

Ah. So *that* was the secret. I could see now how the shooter could have power over the man with the missing toe and make him lie to save the shooter from trouble. I didn't know how these things worked for military men's wives, so I asked. "They won't really have her hanged or shot, will they?"

"Of course not, but she is already packing for her journey back to England. The shooter got off with a warning and was demoted."

"What about the man with the missing toe? Will he face any punishment? Is there a punishment for… for dallying?"

"I doubt if he'll be advancing in the ranks."

"Any names?"

"We have all promised silence and secrecy on this entire matter. But this Ian man who was charged with the crime they claimed he committed and was sentenced to hang for without even having his side heard…" Eliza-Lester was preaching now and I liked it. "… is now free to return to Mirligueche."

"Tell her about the other thing we heard." Bobby squeezed Eliza-Lester's shoulder. "It's even better news."

"Don't you want to tell her that one? I've never met nor had any knowledge of this Dancing Robin person."

"It's *Jumping* Robin and he's called that because he can't dance."

Sofia covered her mouth but her laugh escaped around it.

Bobby stretched himself to his full height, crossed his arms and announced, "They caught him. They caught him spying for both sides. He is now on a ship heading for Louisbourg. And!" He uncrossed his arms and his height lessened. "This is good, too, but hard to hear. He was behind the recent disappearances of many young men between Annapolis Royal and Minas Basin." He turned slightly toward Sofia. "Your area of the land."

"How did we not see this?" I asked.

"My mother knew something like that was going on," said Sofia. "But she didn't dare say a word. Not even to you, Keskoua. And she warned me constantly not to ever, ever say anything about it. Or to even 'see' anything about it. I know that doesn't make any sense, but she told me if I did see it, I must un-see it as fast as possible. And never, ever to say a single word to anyone about it."

Jeune Jean moved closer to Sofia. "The kidnappings? Is that what you're talking about?"

She nodded.

"Who's behind it here then? I'll be back. I have to go talk to somebody."

With that, Jeune Jean disappeared, no longer the apugsign, the lynx, more like the aplíkmuj, the hare.

Twenty-two

Sofia and I were again at the table having tea. No patrons were present because the breakfast meal was over. It would be several hours before the noon meal was announced on the sign near the inn's entrance door.

Bobby was outside in the side yard near the kitchen, helping Chef Georges and Mak get a pig set up over the fire pit. Chef had already removed parts of the pig to start brining hams and bacon so was having trouble balancing it on the spit. I assumed it was going well now as I hadn't heard any cursing or words of complaint for a while.

Eliza-Lester had decided to wander around through the settlement. When I teased her, asking if she were looking for new business, she closed one eye at me and smiled.

And then, Jeune Jean was again coming through the front door into the inn.

"Excellent," he said to Sofia. "You're not busy."

"Not busy? How do you perceive that?"

"Looks like you're just talking."

"And?"

"Well, when women are talking, it's…"

"Yes. It's…?"

"Sorry. Sorry for interrupting. Can I talk to you for a moment?" He motioned for Sofia to move toward the far wall with him. "It's important."

"We can sit here and talk. Anything you tell me, I'll tell her anyway."

At this Jeune Jean laughed then stopped instantly. "Really?"

"Really. Sit."

"By all means, Jeune Jean. Please join us. Would you care for tea?"

"I don't have ti— Uh. Sure. I'll have tea." He sat beside Sofia.

I poured a cup of tea for him and pushed it across the table. He adjusted the handle but made no attempt to drink it.

"I've got something very important to do this afternoon," he said, his face filled with an emotion I had no word for.

I asked him how old he was.

"I'm going to be fourteen."

"I didn't realize you were so young," said Sofia. "When?"

"My next birthday."

"When is that?"

"When it gets here. Listen. I don't have a lot of time. Like I said, I have something important to do this afternoon but after that, I want to come and see you. I want—"

A sudden rumble of boots on the floor and a loud voice calling out made us all jump and turn toward the entranceway.

Guards. Soldiers. With guns pointed at us.

"*All right! Everybody stand in the middle of the room! Everybody out of the kitchen! Now!*"

I had thought no one was in the kitchen so was surprised to see Mak, Chef Georges and Bobby herded like English cows at milking time into the public room by a short, round guard with his musket aimed at their backs.

"I said NOW!"

Twenty-three

I rose from my chair and Jeune Jean helped Sofia out of hers. We joined the others in the middle of the room. I stared at the floor.

Mak slid in beside me on my left. Bobby slid in on my right. Next to him was Sofia, then Jeune Jean. Chef Georges stepped out in front of us.

"We want information," growled one of the guards.

This made me raise my eyes.

As he moved the weapon in his hands upward, I noticed something on his shoulder. It was one of their badges that told the other guards they had to listen to him and do what he wanted. But this wasn't a normal badge. This one was held on by a pin.

That's when I made my eyes look around at the shoulders of the other guards. There was one man standing near the doorway. He held his weapon upwards, to point at the ceiling. I wouldn't say this one was smiling, but I wouldn't say he wasn't either. Behind him, outside, two guards stood talking. It would seem to me that they should have been watching what was going on either inside or outside, but they were doing neither. They were just talking to each other.

As my eyes moved to the shoulders of the other three men, I saw on the one closest to Mak, a dark spot on his shoulder that matched the exact shape of the badge the growling guard wore pinned to his. There were even threads sticking up like the pinfeathers on a duck. This man's face told me he was ashamed and angry. He would bear watching.

As was his usual stance, Georges had his hands behind his back. I saw no clenching of his fists or anything that showed any kind of emotion at all. "You're welcome to any information we might possibly have but if you don't mind, I have a cake in the oven that needs to be tended to."

"And you are?" asked the guard with the pinned-on badge.

"I am Chef Georges. I must return to the kitchen. If my cake burns—even darkens the slightest beyond what I have planned for it—you, my good fellow, will be paying the sum of fifty shillings in recompense. And you will also be apologizing to my supper guests for the absence of it."

The guard glanced over at the man with the threads on his shoulder but got not even a blink of an eye from him. "Uh," he said. "Very well then. But there will be no foolish attempts at escape until we have completed our mission."

"Escape?" I whispered to Mak from the side of my mouth. "Mission?"

"Hush."

At my right, Bobby's voice said the same thing. "Hush."

Georges, arms still behind him, and standing straight and tall, moved around behind us. I heard the shuffle of boots and knew that the short, round guard would be accompanying Georges to the cake in the kitchen.

"Hey," called out the man at the door, his face in full smile. "I have five shillings on me, I'd love some of that cake when it's done."

I recognized his voice. It was the guard who had helped me into Pierre's houseboat the day before. This kind, gentle guard seemed out of place.

"Speak when spoken to, Horace." The guard with the pinned-on badge did not turn around when he said this. Instead, his eyes bore into Bobby's, then Jeune Jean's. "Tell me what went on in here yesterday. I understand there was a meeting."

"Qu'est-ce qu'il a dit, lui? What did he say, him? My English isn't good. Can't understand much of it at all."

Mak spoke. In English. "Apparently there was some kind of meeting went on here yesterday. Do you know anything about that?"

Jeune Jean answered Mak. In English. "I didn't see a damned thing that shouldn't have gone on. What's he talking about?"

"We heard there was a meeting," said the pinned-on-badge guard. "That there were plans being made. Plans that invalidate the peace treaty signed by you people only two months ago."

"Je ne comprend pas l'anglais bien, monsieur. Je m'excuse," said Jeune Jean.

In English, Mak said, "He says they heard there was a meeting. That plans were being made. Plans that would invalidate the peace treaty signed by… He said 'Vous les gens,' 'You people.' And he said a meeting would cause an issue because 'you people' signed the peace treaty."

In English, Jeune Jean said, "Ah. Thank you for translating for me, my friend. Yes. Yes. Of course. The peace treaty. I suppose if we had signed it, we would certainly be abiding by it, yes?"

"I would think so," said Mak. "Did 'you people' sign it?"

"We did."

"Then I guess 'you people' didn't have a meeting then. Did you?"

"I guess not." Here Jeune Jean turned to the guard with the pinned-on badge. "Donc je suppose, puisque nous avons tous signé le traité de paix selon lequel nous n'aurions aucune réunion contre vous, nous n'avons pas eu de réunion à ce moment-là. Avons-nous?"

"What the hell is he nattering on about?" demanded the guard.

I could tell by looking at him, that the guard at the door was doing everything in his power to hold in his laugh. He was shaking his head and looking over at the side of the room where the bar was.

Mak said, in English, "He said, 'So I guess, since we all signed the peace treaty that we wouldn't be having any meetings against you people, we didn't have a meeting then. Did we?"

The guard at the door said, "For Christ's sake, Alvin. Let's go. We aren't going to get anything from these people."

The guard with the pinned-on badge lowered his arms down to his sides. He hung his head and his weapon dangled, barrel down, from his hand. "I suppose you're right. That's it, men. Let's go." He called out toward the kitchen. "Jerry. We're leaving."

Jerry appeared at the doorway of the kitchen with the remains of a piece of cake in his hand. His mouth full, he said, "Mmm. It didn't get burned. It's good. And he gave it to me for nothing. Hey. Wait for me."

The guards had barely gone through the entrance doorway when Eliza-Lester was elbowing her way through them toward me. "Keskoua. Keskoua. Where are—? Ah. There you are. Madame Guédry wants to see you."

"Oh. Is it the baby?"

"Baby? What baby? Oh, not that Madame Guédry. The other Madame Guédry. She said to tell you it's to talk over tea."

When Marguerite wanted to "talk over tea," there was always something serious to be discussed.

Twenty-four

I don't know why it is, but there are some people who, when they hug you, it feels like every care in your soul disappears into the air. Marguerite's hugs were like that.

"Bienvenue. Bienvenue. Come in. Come in. Thank you so much, Lester, for bringing Keskoua to see me. Please be seated. I trust you had no trouble finding her? Tea?" Like a bird's wings as it turns in the sky, her hand moved toward a low, narrow table. On it sat a teapot, napkins, mugs, and plates and spoons and a bowl of what I knew would be maple sugar. Surrounding it, were several chairs and a sofa.

"It's good to see you, Marguerite." I snuggled into Marguerite's sofa among the dozens of pillows there. I think she called them cushions and she had made every one of them. "How is that new grandson of yours?"

Eliza-Lester chose a chair.

"Thanks to young Lester here, the priest will be allowed on their houseboat to baptize young Charles."

"How did you manage that?" I asked.

Before Eliza-Lester could respond, Marguerite pointed to her and said, "This young man has a way about him that commands respect the moment he opens his mouth."

Eliza-Lester was not the only one in the room with that talent. Marguerite was known back home as a woman who was… Shall I use the word insistent? Or the word influential? I knew both from personal experience.

"Instead of using guilt and shame like I do, she uses logic and shame."

We all laughed.

"So the baby's doing fine?" I asked. "And Maggie Deux is fine, as well?"

"I wish you wouldn't call her that, but yes. She's doing fine. And since the birth of the baby, *Maggie Deux* has issued an ultimatum to my son."

Sitting on—it was more like sitting inside—Marguerite's lovely soft sofa with all its cushions would be a wonderful place to nap, but it wasn't the best place to be when you wanted to lean forward and say something. Or take a sip of tea. "She has? How did he take that?" I struggled to sit up straight.

"Not well, of course. To him, moving away would be worse than surrendering. Worse even than failure. Worse than defeat. How did he put it? He said, 'It would be like admitting I was wrong and I'm not.'"

"What did you say? They're moving away? To where?"

"That's the worst of it. The only place they can really go is Louisbourg."

"No. Please tell me that's not true. They'll think he's a spy for sure. That he's been one all along. Maybe they'll take his children away, even though they're Acadians. They aren't even Métis. No, no, no. It's too soon after the birth of the baby for her to be going on any kind of journey. Especially on a houseboat. How can he even think of doing something like that to his wife and family? One of whom is a newborn child!"

"It was her idea, remember?" Marguerite rose from her chair. "I have un déjeuner prepared. A lunch. Care to join me? No, no." She flapped her hand at me. "I'll bring it to you. I know how hard it is to get out of that sofa once you're settled into it." She laughed. "You will note that young Lester here, not only has the ability to influence people when he opens his mouth, but he also has the brains to make good decisions."

"That's not funny," I said, trying once again to sit up straight.

"Yes it is," said Eliza-Lester. To me she said, "She's really funny for an old woman."

From the kitchen: "I heard that. I might be an old woman, but my hearing is fine."

"I'm sorry, Madame Guédry. I didn't mean for you to overhear that."

"Something you must learn," said Marguerite, returning from her kitchen carrying plates of biscuits, cheese, preserved meats and bread, "is never to say anything—anything at all—you don't want someone to overhear."

"Point taken," said Eliza-Lester, snatching a piece of meat off one of the plates. She bit into it. "Ham! Amazing. I haven't had ham for years."

Marguerite raised one eyebrow at me. "Decades, no doubt." She then made her eyes go wide and placed the tips of her fingers over her mouth. "Oh dear. You weren't supposed to overhear that sarcastic remark."

We all laughed.

"So tell me, Marguerite. How will your son ever get the houseboat up to Louisbourg?" I took a bite out of my own ham. I'd wrapped a piece of bread around it. "She's right. This is good. Did you cure the ham yourself?"

"Mon Dieu, no. Why would I go to all that trouble when I have access to a chef from France who can do it ten times better than I could even dream of? I merely supply the pig. He does the work."

"Brilliant," said Eliza-Lester.

"That I am. Right, Keskoua?"

"Do they use the whole pig for ham?" asked Eliza-Lester.

"Heavens, no. They use the belly for bacon and only the arse for ham."

"What!" Eliza-Lester spat into her open palm and her voice went high and feminine when she said. "You're telling me that ham is made out of a pig's arse?"

"You didn't know that?" I asked, trying not to laugh. I pointed at her with my thumb and said to Marguerite, "She didn't know that. I can't believe it."

"Wait." Marguerite turned toward Eliza-Lester. "She said she. I'm sorry, are you two-spirited? Should I be saying she and not he?"

"No, she's not two-spirited. She has ambitions and she's female."

"Aha. Even smarter than I thought she was, he was. Sorry."

"It's something I'm going to have to get used to, I'm afraid. I'm going to Boston. I've already studied Law but I want to study more of it."

"I see."

"As a female, I could study enough Law to be able to teach the most learned judge, but all I could ever be is a court reporter. If I am male, I can be a lawyer. Which is what I want to be."

Marguerite smiled at me. "Smarter than smarter than I thought."

"Speaking of smart," said Eliza-Lester. "Louisbourg, you said? How does your son plan to get there? In a houseboat of all things. I imagine he's the one…" Here she raised her eyebrows at me. "… the one who isn't allowed to touch foot on English soil?"

I nodded and took another bite out of my folded bread and ham. "You realize, of course, that ham is not made out of the actual hole in the pig's arse, or from what's inside there. Right?" I controlled my laughter and so did Marguerite. "It's actually the pig's hip. Marguerite was joking."

"Well I *am* hungry." She reached for the rest of her ham and took a bite. "Taste out-rules everything when you're hungry," she said while chewing, and without making a face. "So, Madame Guédry—"

"Please. Marguerite. Or, if you wish, Mamaw."

"All right, Mamaw. How does your son plan to get his wife and young family to Louisbourg on a houseboat? It can be dangerous on a *ship* if the weather changes. Or if some idiot thinks they're a pirate ship or the enemy. But traveling any distance by houseboat? Pure foolishness."

"My son is not a fool."

"I didn't mean it that way. I meant—"

"They'll be taking him."

"They?" said Eliza-Lester and I at the same time.

"They. The Maudits anglaises." Marguerite smiled with pride. "And they have even set up a system of making bids for the purchase of his houseboat. And he will get the money."

"They must want him gone badly," I said.

"They do. They say he's a bad influence."

"A bad influence? No!" Eliza-Lester didn't pound her fist on anything, but her words and face did. "He's been a *positive* influence. A positive influence for going against what's happening here recently. Your children and grandchildren are doing the right thing in trying to insist on fair treatment."

"It's so dangerous, though." Marguerite set her half-eaten ham down on her napkin. I noticed she had also folded bread around it. "Morning Star came to see me at daybreak."

"Morning Star?" asked Eliza-Lester.

"J-B's wife. She's worried. Not only about him, but about her brothers as well. They're… How did she say it? 'They're cooking a stew of something that doesn't belong in a stew.' She's frantic with worry."

"What's going on?" I asked. "I haven't seen J-B since I arrived here. I go somewhere only to find I just missed him."

"She said he has harvested the entire farm's fields. He spent most of yesterday tying bales of straw and hay for winter storage. The silo is full. She's got me worried now, too, mon Dieu. I know it's near the end of August, so it's time for some harvesting, but she says he's preparing all the straw and hay for winter." She turned to Eliza-Lester. "We're usually more relaxed about it. We have all of September and usually part of October to do that. She says he burned through two lamps overnight chopping wood. The woodpile reaches the roofline now, she says."

"Do you think he got into the maple sugar?" I was trying to make a joke, trying to lessen Marguerite's worrying. That was the way of our people. We liked to laugh, especially when situations were serious. It helped us keep our minds in the right place so we could solve problems more quickly.

It was as though she hadn't heard me. "She also says that her brother James has become a worry to J-B. Thus to her as well. James, she says, is delirious with worry and grief about their brother, François. J-B is afraid James is going to do something everyone will regret."

"François?" asked Eliza-Lester. "That's the other boy who was taken with young Paul, is it not?"

"Yes," I said. "He would be about fifteen now. Paul's eleven."

It was as though Marguerite hadn't heard this either. "James, they say, has become unstable. Especially now that they're handing out rum to anyone who comes on board searching for wares in exchange for goods. The New Englanders who fish here are becoming angry when their knives, clothing and money are being taken in exchange for what we provide to them. Are these things not a fair exchange in their world, too? Especially the money? Are they not?"

This time, I was the one who didn't respond to a question. I knew the answer. And Marguerite knew I knew the answer. She needed to get the anger out of herself by talking. Talking was always good.

"Suddenly, money in exchange for goods and services is not accepted? They want to give them rum instead? No. This is wrong."

"I always say, I will never understand the English."

"I think the Scots are beginning to agree with you. This is supposed to be their land now. Given to them by England. Even they are having trouble fishing without the New Englanders trying to stop them from doing so. Who gave permission for the New Englanders to invade our land and steal our fish?"

"And our children." I said quietly. "They take any young Mi´gmaw children they catch fishing. They take them away."

"As I well know!" Marguerite said. "They put them in prison, oui? That's where they are?"

"No. It's not where they are and you know that, Marguerite. You know exactly where they are."

"Mon Dieu. Don't tell me that. I don't want to know that. I don't want to think that. Not about my grandson! Let's go back to talking about rum. The damned rum that's ruining not only your people but our young ones as well. Oh mon Dieu, help me stop thinking about my grandson." She took a sip of tea, took a deep breath then continued. "It's fine to have a glass to help us sleep. Or wine with a meal or to cook with but... What do you think of this, Lester? Or do you prefer to be called Eliza?" Marguerite seemed to be calming down.

"Lester."

"Are they handing out rum in the hopes the young people will become dependent on it? And then they can sell that to them, too, and make even more money off us?"

"Sounds about right," said Eliza-Lester.

"What's it like," I asked them.

Eliza-Lester turned her eyes away from me to something on the wall behind Marguerite. "What's what like?"

Marguerite noticed this, too, and her eyes met mine. "You get relaxed and if you have too much, any rules—even the Commandments of God—disappear from your conscience. Nothing seems wrong anymore. I think it's easier for some to become attached to—"

A sound from the porch stopped her from saying more.

"Who's there. Who's out there. Speak, or be shot."

A man's laughter drifted in. "Don't shoot. It's me. Your friend Samuel."

Marguerite's face lit up. She rose from her chair. "It's Captain Doty. From the *Tryal*."

"Trial?"

Marguerite chuckled. "A lawyer for sure. Not that kind of trial, Lester. It's the name of his sloop and it's spelled with a y."

Carrying a large cloth bag, the man appeared and went directly to Marguerite. They hugged briefly. He was medium in height and had a kind, weathered face.

She flipped her hand at Eliza-Lester telling her to let Captain Doty have her chair.

Eliza-Lester moved to sit beside me on the sofa, and as she did, she cried out, "Oh my. It's like being sucked into the siphon of a clam!"

I patted her knee. This girl was smart indeed. Meet the captain of a fishing sloop? Establish instant trust by leading him to think you know something about fishing. Anything about fishing would do. I had tried that ruse myself.

Captain Doty handed the cloth bag to Marguerite. "Books and yarn for you." He sat and smiled at the plates there. Then smiled at Eliza-Lester. Then at me. I thought I could smell spirits on his breath. "And I see that our lunch is already before us and you didn't even know I was coming."

"I'll make you a cup of my special tea. Mon spéciali-*thé*," Marguerite removed her mug from the table and off she went to the kitchen.

"Sounds wonderful," said Captain Doty as he picked up one of the pieces of ham and a slice of bread from the table. "Ham. I so enjoy ham. Has she pulled that ham joke on you yet? The one about the pig's arse?" He called out after her: "Oh, and Marguerite. If you hear any noises outside or see anything going on, my crew are just filling the water jugs at your well. It's only Silas and Nathaniel. The others have gone elsewhere for other supplies."

"Oh, my dear friend Samuel. I owe you more than water for these books. And it just so happens that I have preserves in the fruit cellar. I just did up some honeyed strawberries. Want me to bring some up for you?"

"That would be wonderful. Thank you."

"I'll do it," I said. "I know my way around the house. Unless you've changed things since my last visit?"

"The strawberry jam is where it always is, dear. And thank you. Three for him. Take one for yourself."

I managed, with the help of Captain Doty's strong hand and arm, to get myself out of… What had Eliza-Lester called it? Out of that clam of a couch.

Twenty-five

I brought up four jars of honeyed strawberry jam from the fruit cellar that led off the kitchen into a cave-like room below. It always amazed me how much cooler it was down there and I loved the smell. It smelled like milk.

I hadn't been down below for very long but by the time I got back upstairs to join everyone again, I learned that Eliza-Lester had already tried to book passage with Captain Doty for Boston.

Eliza-Lester was insisting, because Captain Doty's home was in Plymouth, so he would have to pass by Boston on the way, there was no reason she couldn't come along. She could pay the fare. Even a higher one, just to be able to get there sooner. She would not have to go to Louisbourg after all if she could go with him right now.

"But there's a problem, you see," said Captain Doty. "Please. Marguerite. I'm fine. Please be seated. There's a rather serious matter needs discussing."

I set the jars of jam on the center of the table and as I did so, I was leaning over near Captain Doty's tea mug. That was not tea in his mug. That was some kind of spirits. Perhaps mulled wine. Passing behind Marguerite's chair told me her mug held no tea either. I smiled and said nothing.

"But what about your boys?" she said. "Wouldn't they like to visit?

Have some of my special tea? Nathaniel likes my special tea." She stood up again and headed toward the front door. "I'll go ask."

"Marguerite!" This he said in a harsh voice. "Get back here. Sit. Something serious is going on and we need to discuss it. J-B came on board this morning. At my bequest but with no hesitation. He's still there. Jeune Jean brought him aside in a canoe." Captain Doty pronounced Jeune Jean like June John.

Face pale and eyes wide, Marguerite returned. She slumped into her chair. "Please tell me he's not."

"I wish I could tell you he's not. But he is. He has a plan. It could work. But his… The others… They can't be trusted. Especially James. He was on board the moment we dropped anchor and got away with two bottles of rum. Without, I might add, my permission."

"Oh, mon Dieu, mon Dieu. Merde. Please don't say anything to the authorities."

"Well, it's not entirely his fault about that, you know. Any time he comes on board—onto any ship, I hear—he asks for and is given a bottle of rum. No question. I suppose he just assumed one would be his. But now…"

"Two bottles you say."

"Two."

"And why did you wish to speak to J-B? Why did you call him on board? What did you talk about?"

"We talked about the peace treaty. The one signed in June. The one that no one in this area seems to be abiding by."

"And why would we?" said Marguerite, her lips squeezed into a tiny circle. "That was no more a treaty than a dollop of bird droppings on a rock. One side: Don't fight against us anymore. The other side? No changes whatsoever. Did he tell you they still have not released my grandson? Nor the brother of James whom you refer to as 'trouble' as though he has nothing to be troubled about?"

"I understand all that," said Captain Doty. "The problem is… The problem is, James wants to take control of any New England ships or sloops that come into port here. J-B confided in me that he is very concerned about this, but says he has no choice but to go along with the idea. They plan to maintain that control until those boys are released from… Well. From wherever they are." Here, Captain Doty looked over at me. "I think you know that those children—and the others who apparently 'disappear'—are not being held in a Boston prison."

I nodded and I felt the sofa's cushions under my elbow move slightly as Eliza-Lester must have nodded, too.

Captain Doty continued, his eyes not wavering from the plate of biscuits, cheeses, preserved meats and bread. I now had an idea of what he might have been trying to tell Marguerite. I wouldn't have wanted to be looking into her eyes either. "That's the last thing anyone should do. Especially with only a handful of men. It would be…" Here, his eyes did meet hers.

"Are you saying they are planning to become pirates? Are they insane? That's certain death!"

"It seems they are willing to risk it to get their family out of… Out of the situation their family members are in. And other people's family members, too. They're willing to lead a revolt of sorts to get the children released."

"I don't blame them," I said. "My husband Mak is from Africa. He came over on one of the slave ships. We managed to get him directly away from Boston Harbor soon after he landed, so he knows something of being on the wrong side of slavery… And of course, many African people are here now, in the area. Some of them are able to tell of their… their experiences."

"I'm aware. Yes."

I glanced over at Marguerite who had her fingers in her ears. "Mon dieu, mon dieu. S'il vous plaît, arrêtez. Please stop. I don't want to hear anything of this!"

"As far as J-B is concerned, there *is* peace. But he is losing hope that they will return his son and young brother-in-law. He is ready to take steps. But only if he has to. You see, J-B is not entirely behind the plans of his brothers-in-law, who, sadly, have convinced Jeune Jean to go along with their ideas."

"He's at that age," I said. "They think they know everything when they arrive at fourteen winters."

"He's not there, yet," Marguerite corrected me.

"Perhaps he's practicing?"

There I was, trying to lighten things again, but I felt bad about it as soon as the words were out of my mouth even though I was happy to see a small smile forming on Marguerite's face.

"Jeune Jean came aboard then, and as I spoke, I thought I was perhaps beginning to get through to him at least, but a shout from shore—I'm not sure from whom, James or perhaps Philippe—caused him to leave my sloop. There were several men gathered there. A woman and two children, as well.

"After we spoke at some length, I told J-B that I and my crew had to go ashore for supplies. He was reluctant to get into my small boat with so many already in it. I told him he was welcome to stay, that he could help himself to more wine if he wished. He would do that, he told me, as soon as he finished the glass of wine I'd already given him. He told me also that he would call out to Jeune Jean to come get him later. And here I am, supposedly enjoying tea with you, and he is on my sloop enjoying wine with the one crew member left on board, Sachimus."

"I believe they know each other," said Marguerite.

"I believe they do so will have a grand old conversation about this and that. For me now, though, my dear lady, Missus Guédry..." He pronounced it Giddery. "I must be on my way." He rose from his chair and bowed slightly to me. "Pleased to make your acquaintance, madam.

I have enjoyed your company. And…" to Eliza-Lester, "… young man, if anything happens to make the current situation more amenable to your getting to Boston by means of my sloop, I will send a message. Is that acceptable?"

"Thank you, Captain. Most assuredly, it is."

No sooner had these words come out from Eliza-Lester's lips, than distant shouts sounded.

"What the hell's going on?" Captain Doty took off at a full run.

Eliza-Lester was right behind him. Marguerite and I followed as fast as we could.

Twenty-six

On shore stood a group of men, women and children. Four of the men I did not know. One of them, not much more than a boy, was one of our people. The way Captain Doty spoke to them, though, made me realize they were his crew.

Something moved my eyes toward two places.

The first place was on my left where a man was climbing up the mast of a ship and he was having a difficult time doing it. From the shouts going back and forth between him and a man at the rail, it looked as though he wasn't trained to do it. When the climbing man saw me looking at him, he waved. "It's me. Bobby."

"Careful," I called back.

"He's done it afore," called the man at the rail. "Don't worry. My friend here can do anything. Or so he told me."

There was laughter but not from me or those beside me.

The second place my eyes went to was where Bobby was now pointing. To a sloop with the name *Tryal* on its bow. "That's your sloop," I said to Captain Doty.

Marguerite, out of breath, answered for me. "It is." Beside her was another of her sons, Augustin. He was supporting her by her elbow. He was out of breath, too. He must have run to catch up to us.

I saw Jeune Jean, James and Philippe wave from the rail of the *Tryal.*

Then Philippe disappeared from the rail.

"Bien merde," called Bobby. "He's striking the colors. Oh, no." He shouted over at the men on the *Tryal*. "Philippe! Stop. Don't do that!"

"What's that mean?" my mouth asked anyone who might be listening to me.

"God damn him," said Captain Doty, suddenly at my side.

"What's going on? What did he do? What does it mean to strike the colors?"

"This is not good." He turned to me. "It means to lower the flag. They have no right to do this without my permission. I don't like what they're doing. This is not good. Not good."

Behind us, a gunshot.

I turned, but no one was moving or looking at anyone. I couldn't tell who had fired it.

A gunshot answered from the sloop. A voice from the sloop called out. I couldn't tell who said it, but I thought perhaps James or Philippe. "*CALL TO QUARTERS!*"

Bobby called out. "The flag is down. Philippe is… It looks like he's cutting it up with his knife. No. Wait. J-B took it from him. Can't hear what he said but J-B is taking the flag from him and… He's wrapping it around his own waist."

"Thank God for that, at least," said Captain Doty. "But still very bad."

"And now… They're tying somebody up. And J-B has taken the man's pistol from James. Yes. And now J-B is putting the pistol into the flag around his waist."

Captain Doty turned to speak to his men. "We have to get on board." Then he called out the same to J-B who was now at the rail.

J-B called back, "I'm sending Sachimus to get you, Samuel. I am setting him loose."

"Now there's a big argument going on," called Bobby. "Looks like

James doesn't want J-B untying that man. Oh. That was close! James took a swing at J-B with his hatchet. Philippe is trying to break them apart. No. James took another swing. Oh no. He's not going to be happy about this." Bobby laughed.

"Why? What? What happened?"

Still laughing, Bobby said, "When James swung at him, he did it with full power. But J-B jumped out of the way and this sent James spinning across the deck. He appears to be very drunk."

"That's it," said Eliza-Lester. "I'm coming on board with you, Captain. I think I can help solve this problem. I'll be right back." She was gone.

Bobby called out, "James is down. He's not moving. Oh, wait. Yes. He just rolled over onto his back. Philippe has taken the hatchet from him. And now, James is lying there laughing. All is well."

But all was not well. Salmon and Young Dove Man were paddling a canoe at full speed toward the sloop and calling out, "We're on our way, James. We're coming to help. We're coming to help."

In another canoe following behind them, but at a much slower pace, was Lobster and with him was a woman. His wife? And two children. *His* children? What was he thinking? "I'm on my way, too, James."

"James is on his feet again but none too steady."

Hurry back, Eliza-Lester.

At the *Tryal* now, a man was being lowered to a wooden boat. This must be the one called Sachimus. The one they'd tied up and J-B had released.

Then James jumped up onto the rail. I wasn't certain what I heard but it sounded like, "*There is peace with the Indians.*" Was it a question or a statement? I couldn't tell. He said it in English and I knew his English was poor to nonexistent.

It seemed to take forever for Sachimus to reach shore with the wooden boat but I was happy about that. Eliza-Lester hadn't returned yet. Sachimus jumped out of it and pulled it up so Captain Doty could get into it without getting his feet wet.

Captain Doty had one foot inside the boat, when a breathless Eliza-Lester, trying to keep a large woven sack from sliding off her shoulder, almost ran into the water beside him.

"I'm coming with you whether you like it or not. I can help."

Sachimus paused for the briefest time before lifting the sack from her arms. He grunted. "What do you have in this thing?"

I could see from here that she had stuffed books and papers into it. Probably clothing, too, as I could see the sleeve of a garment hanging out of it.

"Things I need." With the help of Captain Doty, she climbed in. "Thank you, sir."

Sachimus swung her luggage toward Captain Doty who nearly lost his balance when he caught it. "I hope all of this is necessary?"

"It is," she said. "Let's go."

Little did any of us know that we would never again see J-B, or Jeune Jean, or James, or Philippe, or John Missel, or Salmon, or Young Dove Man, or J-B's lost son, Paul, or François, the young brother of James and Philippe, or even the wife of Lobster, or his children. But Lobster himself showed up at our inn three days later.

It was early morning. There had been a heavy fog and it had not yet lifted. As silent as a thief, Lobster entered.

"Go get Madame Guédry," he whispered, trying to catch his breath like he had been running for hours. "She has to hear everything that happened. We need a Sacred Fire. Then I will need the Sweat Lodge." He collapsed onto the floor.

Twenty-seven

"Once James gets something into his head, nobody can get it out," Lobster told Mak and me. "Thank you." He took the mug of tea that Sofia was holding out to him.

To me, he said, "I'm sorry I frightened you."

"We thought you were dead. Drowned. That's what they told us."

"I thought I was dead, too. I wish I were dead. My wife. My children. Gone. And It's my fault. I…" Lobster moaned and his hand went to the side of his head. I hadn't noticed the cut and the lump.

"Let me look at that." I swung my munti off my shoulder and began hunting through it. "What happened? Did you bump your head? Or was it bumped for you?"

I could hear excited voices and noises out in the side yard. The banging of wood against wood told me a fire was being prepared.

"Bumped *for* me, I think. *Aie.*" I had pulled some of Lobster's hair away from his wound to better see it.

"This might sting," I said as I applied ointment to his wound. "But it will keep the microbes out."

"Let the bastards in. I don't care if I die. My wife and children are dead. The last thing I remember is seeing their faces through a little round window as I fell into the water."

"Who struck you?"

"I don't know. All I remember is floating on my back as the sloop sped away and my wife's face… Then I was on a ship. A French ship, I think. It must have been. I don't remember having trouble understanding them when they spoke to me. So yes. French. Then I don't remember anything much after that. I guess they fished me out of the water? Brought me here? I remember waking up lying on shore. But I was covered with a blanket so I know I didn't float in with the tide like a dead…" Here, he laughed but not with humor, "… a dead Lobster?"

"We heard that you, Salmon and Young Dove Man were all drowned," said Mak. "Bobby heard that. He didn't say who it was told him, though."

"Nor *will* I," said Bobby.

Mak glanced over at him, then continued, "In fact, as I think of it, he refused even to tell me what day he heard it."

"It must have been one of the men from the French ship. One of those who saved me. They can't tell anyone they were a party to saving me. Or they, too, will face the gallows. Like I will be doing when they learn I am still alive."

"No one needs to know," said Mak, heading for the inn's entrance door. "I'll be right back." At the door, he paused. "Keskoua?"

"Yes?"

"Get him onto the floor. Lobster?"

Lobster frowned at him.

"Pretend you *are* that dead lobster who floated onto the shore."

As I helped Lobster get off his chair, I heard Mak's voice from among the excited voices outside. I couldn't hear his words but from his tone, I knew he was informing the crowd of bad news. I heard moans. I heard the clatter of wood being dropped on top of wood.

Mak's head appeared at the doorway. "I shall go collect Marguerite." Then he called out toward the kitchen. "Sofia. We need only one pot of tea for now. Relax. We're closing the inn until the evening meal."

"Dear Lord above," came Sofia's voice. "Does no one ever make up one's mind around here?"

"Oh. And something to nibble on. A plate of those things Georges calls Off Course."

Sofia's face appeared at the kitchen's door. "You're supposed to use the actual French words for those. Hors d'oeuvres. Means outside the work." Her eyes widened. "Oh! Is that man dead?"

I was in the process of laying Lobster onto the floor. He was giving an excellent performance as a dead Lobster.

"Oh, sorry. I… All right. One pot of tea it is, then."

"If anyone asks. Yes. He died."

"That's too bad."

"But he'll still need a mug for tea."

I heard Sofia mutter something as her head disappeared from view. "I will never understand these people."

Twenty-eight

"Once Captain Doty came on board," said Lobster. "He was approached by James who snatched the captain's hat from him, put it on himself, and declared, loudly, "Now I am captain of the vessel. Call your men on board or I'll send my men ashore and kill them all."

Even though she tried to keep it in, I could hear Marguerite's gasp from my end of the big table near the long bar, the table where, only a few days earlier, the very men we were talking about had sat discussing their plans. Beside her, Bobby patted her arm.

"Captain Doty waved. 'Did you hear that, men? Come on board.'

"James was standing behind him with a hatchet in his hand. I don't know where it came from. I still had mine, so he didn't take mine. I checked. He shouted, 'Peace proclaimed? I will never make peace with the English until the governor of Boston releases my brother and the son of my sister. Never!'

"Here, he raised his fist into the air. 'I'll burn every New England ship and sloop that comes near until that is done.'

"This was unexpected," said Lobster, his eyes lowered. "We had discussed this. Let's say, James had discussed this and often, but we had always convinced him otherwise. It would mean certain death. We..." Lobster reached for his mug of tea to sip the last drop from it.

I hadn't even noticed Sofia standing behind me, but she was right there, to top up Lobster's mug. He was between me and Mak. Georges sat halfway along the side of the long table, arranging and rearranging the… What were they called? *Outside the work?* No. Hors d'oeuvres. Over and over again. It wasn't difficult to see that he was concerned.

"Almost immediately, the rest of Captain Doty's men were in canoes and small boats and heading for the sloop. By this time, Jeune Jean had come up from his searchings below with as many bottles of rum as he could carry. He set them on the floor—"

"It's called the deck," I said. Then covered my mouth. "Sorry." *Don't interrupt when someone is speaking.*

"The deck. Thank you, Keskoua." He smiled at me. "It's perfectly all right to correct me. My mind is not all that clear and my head hurts. I hope I am able to recall everything. If I don't…" He looked down the table at Marguerite, "… please forgive me."

"Of course, dear. Of course."

"But this is where you come in."

"Me?" Marguerite pointed at her chest. "Oh, yes. Yes. Me." Eyes pointed downward, she shook her head. "I failed. I was unable to convince them to stop."

Lobster said, "You did your best, Mamaw. You did your best."

She took the handkerchief Bobby was holding out to her and wiped her eyes and her nose with it. "My best was not even close to good enough."

Bobby put his arm across Marguerite's back. "You tried, Mamaw. You tried. That's all you could have done. Their minds were made up."

"Please," she said to Lobster. "Continue."

"Jeune Jean actually tipped up a bottle of rum and drank it as though it were water," Lobster said. "J-B cried out to him to stop drinking it like that, but Jeune Jean just laughed and he and James put their arms around each other and tipped up the bottles again. They called out, 'We will see our brothers again. We will see our brothers again.' I would say, within minutes, they were both heavily asleep on the fl— on the deck." Lobster's sad eyes looked into mine.

"Before long—and I admit to my own guilt at this—we were all consuming rum and going through the stores of the sloop. Philippe even went through the captain's pockets, with his clothes still on him, and here I mean Captain Doty, not 'Captain James'! Therein, he found seventeen shillings. Someone, I don't know who, perhaps my wife, brought up cheese and other provisions from below and handed it out to everyone. Somehow, J-B ended up with rings and a belt buckle. Valuable ones as far as I could tell. Captain Doty told him to put them back and the way he said it make me think he was trying to help J-B. But by then…" Lobster took another sip of tea.

"My memory of events is not clear after that. But I do remember J-B telling the crew to hoist the anchor and set sail. He was now the new captain since our 'Captain James' was passed out from the rum. J-B thought it great fun. I'm not sure he realized the seriousness of everything that was going on. Rum dumbs, I always say. I do know that the crew did not follow the orders of this particular captain, though. By the sun, then later, by the stars, I knew we were going in circles. Slow circles. Heading out, yes, but without making any headway.

"Then somehow, we got the captain and his men locked below and all night we ate and drank and enjoyed ourselves up on deck. We must have dropped anchor." Lobster paused and his eyebrows squeezed together. "We must have. Everyone who knew how to steer the sloop was below. I don't think, drunk as we all were, we would have let ourselves drift… Darkness came, clouds obscured the moon. Ah, I remember now. We lit candles." He laughed. "We had a Sacred Fire made out of candles. Can you imagine? When I think of it now… How foolish we all were…"

Georges slid the tray of hors d'oeuvres toward our end of the table. Each of us plucked a piece of meat or cheese or biscuit from it. With his fingertips, Georges then slid the tray to the other end of the table. Bobby took something. Marguerite did not.

"Morning came and of course, we were all feeling the rum from the night before. Except for James, we were all awake but not so much aware. However, we did spot a schooner coming toward us. Thinking it was an English schooner coming to attack us, we did our best to prepare for them. We found guns, powder and shot. I remember something about fishing nets and the bits of lead in them. I think we assumed they would act as ammunition for the small arms we found. I think it was John Missel found those and suggested their use.

"I must apologize for not being able to recall things as clearly as you might wish, Mamaw."

"You are doing just fine, dear," said Marguerite. "May I have more tea, Sofia. Please?"

At this, everyone reached into the plate on the table for more hors d'oeuvres as Sofia went around the table topping up everyone's tea.

"I'll be right back with fresh," she said.

But no sooner had she stepped away from the table when I heard a rattling at the locked doorway to the inn. Someone was trying to enter.

Twenty-nine

A banging at the door preceded a shout. "Is Keskoua in there? I have something for her."

"It's the guard who got his foot shot off," Sofia whispered to us as loudly as she could.

"Quick," I said. "Time to play dead again, Lobster. Get up on the table. Everyone circle around and look like you're praying or something."

Chairs squeaked behind me as I headed for the door.

"Go get the tea," I told Sofia. "Pretend that nothing is any different from normal."

"Dear Lord above."

I glanced over at the table before I reached down to unlock and open the doorway. Lobster was once again playing Dead Lobster on the table and the others were looking down at him. Even Marguerite was in on it as she was wiping her eyes. Georges looked his same serious self. Bobby was covering his mouth with both hands.

I opened the door. "Good morning. I'm sor—" It was the man who had helped me into Pierre's houseboat when Maggie Deux was about to have her baby. It was the same man who had stood at the door a few days earlier, trying not to laugh while we were being questioned by the guard with the badge pinned on his shoulder. This was the man who'd had his toe shot off? The man who had "dallied" with his superior officer's wife? "We aren't open yet and won't be for a while." I said "sorry" and I meant it.

"I have something for you." He held out a tiny folded paper package. "Pigeon message. Just in."

"Oh." I took it from him. "Is it something important?"

"I… I don't know, ma'am. I didn't read it." His eyes told me otherwise.

"Thank you, kind sir." And I pushed him and his advancing boot backwards, shut the door and turned the key in the lock.

He remained standing at the door, staring at me through its window.

I slid the curtains over, smiling at him as I did so.

I opened the message and knew immediately it was from Eliza-Lester.

Convinced new friend stop La Hève to leave two packages of roe and the one who produced these packages at the home of Aunt Willow.

"I think I might have some good news," I said, heading toward the table, waving the paper, and trying to control my excitement.

Lobster still lay there, quiet, unmoving. I could barely see his chest moving up and down. He was an excellent actor.

"Lobster? You can resurrect yourself now. He's gone."

I looked down at him. He opened one eye. "I think I like being dead. No worries when you're dead."

"Well I think you're going to have to come alive and be healthy soon because you are going on a journey. And I don't mean the big Journey. I mean an overland journey. To La Hève."

He sat up and swung his legs around and off the table. Sofia was right there to wipe it off with her towel. Georges grabbed the plate of hors d'oeuvres off the bar and put it back onto the table. He motioned for Sofia to replace the mugs and see to filling them.

"Tell us," said Mak. "Don't keep us in suspense. What does the message say? Who's it from?"

"It's from uh… It's from Lester. And it contains a mystery. A puzzle. A secret message."

"What does it say?" Lobster snatched the paper from me and looked at it. "Uh." His face went red as he handed it back to me. "I forgot. I can't read."

I decided it would be fun to tease everyone, especially Lobster. "Where does roe come from?"

"Salmon," said Bobby. "Everybody knows that."

"It's in regular fish, too," said Marguerite.

Georges was laughing. "They're safe?" he asked.

"All three," I told him. "Come on. What else produces roe?"

Lobster threw his arms around Bobby who was the closest to him right then. "Does it say that? Does it say that?"

I read the note aloud.

Lobster's eyes flooded with water. "They're safe? They're in La Hève? Does that guy really have an aunt there?"

"I know the answer to that one," said Bobby. "Aunt Willow is not a real person. But there is a woman who runs an inn, much like this one, but with special rooms in it for special people who don't want to be found. If you know what I mean."

Lobster hugged Bobby again, then he hugged me, then Mak, then Georges then Marguerite. Sofia had disappeared back into the kitchen.

Once the excitement of the good news had settled down, Lobster continued with the events that had taken two of his friends to their immediate death and five of his friends to their probable death.

"Like I said, the next morning we saw a schooner that we were certain was an English one. James was passed out but still muttering about 'killing all the English bastards and burning their ships,' and Philippe was drunk enough to be agreeing with him. But not J-B. J-B ordered, as the non-captain he was, that we set sail instead, for his farm. I'm sure he was trying his best to avoid any confrontation with a heavily armed English ship, one that could very well be seeking us. But at this point, who knew what was in anyone else's mind?

"As it turned out, when it got close enough to us, we could see that it was a French vessel. I must say, I was not the least bit disappointed with this news. We all relaxed. And relaxing was our downfall. What followed was a confusing turmoil. Perhaps because of the blow to my head and the effects of having had too much rum the night before already in my system, I don't recall everything that happened." Once more, his eyes sought Marguerite's.

"I do remember seeing John Missel at the rail, fishing. The crew was doing what crews do, I suppose. They were on deck. Then Salmon and Young Dove Man were thrown below where my wife and children were. J-B went overboard. Then everyone was everywhere and I…

"I heard splashing. Then John Missel cried out, 'Salmon and his boy have got through the window. They're in the water. They're going under! They're going under. Help them.'

"We ran to the rail and looked over. J-B was able to swim and he swam toward them but it was too late. They disappeared just as he got to them. The wail that came from his mouth I will never forget." He looked down the table at Marguerite. "He tried, Mamaw. He tried to save them."

Marguerite dabbed at her eyes again but this time, there were real tears there.

"Then from behind us, the crew attacked and I don't really remember what happened after that. Except waking up floating on my back on the water. I saw J-B struggling to climb into a canoe that was attached to the sloop. I don't know why it was attached there. Ah, yes. I remember now. Philippe had lowered it so we could approach the English schooner before they got to us. To give us the advantage. Yes. It's starting to come back. But I'm sorry. Not everything, though. J-B got himself into the canoe and the last I saw, he was hauling himself up a ladder. John Missel was at the top of the ladder. Then everything is foggy again.

"I'm so sorry, Mamaw. I can't remember anything after that. All I know is, they were all arrested. And this I know from the young boy who found me on the shore and kicked me awake this morning. I'm sure he'll be having cauchemars tonight. I thought he was going to drop dead of fright when I sat up. Maybe this story will be funny to him some day. But it certainly isn't to me."

"I'm sorry," I said. "Let's get you ready for your journey. I'm certain your wife must be frantic with worry. And you cannot be found here."

"I'll go with him," said Bobby. "I've done the overland from here to there before."

Thirty

Within a few days I received another pigeon message from Eliza-Lester. This one, she did not write in code.

She had arrived safely and had made her connection with Edward Gooden, assuring me that he would be no problem in any way as he had found himself yet another wife. Here, she had drawn a laughing face. Then wrote the question: "Why would you think this extremely elderly man…" over eighty now, I just then realized, "… could ever tempt me into committing any kind of indiscretion."

This made me laugh.

That was our way. To use humor to lighten situations that were difficult to face.

When I lifted off that section of the pigeon message to read the second page, I knew what was written there would be bad. And it was. It was very bad. Not only would J-B, Jeune Jean, James, Philippe and John Missel be tried in Boston court for theft of goods, but because the ship, while under their command, and unknown to them, had strayed into waters that were out of bounds, they would be tried for something much worse.

Eliza-Lester suggested to me that perhaps Captain Doty's crew had been able, somehow, to do this on purpose without being found out. Their purpose being that the men would be charged with piracy. And hanged for it. Lobster had noticed they'd been going in circles, but had thought nothing of it.

On October 6, the day after the trial, I received the dreaded pigeon message from Eliza-Lester asking me to give the news wrapped within it to Marguerite. Once again, there were two pages to the message: one for me and one for my dear friend, Marguerite Petitpas, Missus Guédry. Marguerite and I together would pass the news to Morning Star.

Everyone had told the truth, Eliza-Lester assured me. And I knew of her understanding of many languages so could trust her to be knowing if it was the truth or not. This would not, of course, make Marguerite feel any better. Her son and grandson were found guilty of piracy as were the Mius brothers and John Missel.

J-B had argued and pled with the Court that his son was not yet fourteen years old.

He had begged them not to hang him.

They had refused.

They would be hanged within weeks.

In November.

And they were.

Thirty-one

Bobby had no trouble getting Lobster to La Hève and his family. From there, they were able to get passage with… so I heard… Captain Richard to Annapolis Royal. Bobby would tell me no more about their plans but somehow I knew they would end up meeting my friend Agada and the Littles and all the others who lived between Annapolis Royal and Minas Basin.

***

No one was surprised when Sofia changed her mind about going to Boston. She soon became an important part of Mak's and my Mirligueche inn. She and Chef Georges became close, he like a father figure, as he taught her everything he knew about French cooking.

Bobby was delighted about this opportunity to woo Sofia.

"I didn't change my mind about going away to Boston so I could be with you," she snapped at him. "My heart is still breaking for Jeune Jean, even though he was just a child. He liked me and I liked him."

But within months, Bobby and Sofia were married and a baby was on the way.

Agada's baby arrived safely and she and Ian were married, too, much to Sofia's embarrassment. "Dear Lord above, whose mother gets married the same year her daughter does? And has a baby, too. It's disgusting."

"I think it's sweet," I said.

"*Mor* always told me you were weird and I didn't believe her. But now I do."

***

Pierre Guédry dit LaBine and his family made it safely to Louisbourg and no one was happier about that than Maggie Deux. We kept in touch for a while but then lost track of each other.

***

It took us all a long time to recover from these changes. Marguerite never recovered. She passed away in her sleep two years later.

***

Life would be relatively uneventful for everyone during the next couple of decades but…

What's that expression about the calm before the storm?

Terrible things would once again happen to the people of l'Acadie, to the Acadians and especially to the Métis, the Mixed.

But I'm getting ahead of myself again, aren't I?

Acknowledgments

Special thanks go to Phyllis Bohonis, Sue Pictou and the Online Talking Dictionary: www.mikmaqonline.org/.

About the Author

Sherrill Wark edits and designs print/digital books for indie authors under the banners of Crowe Creations (general) and Ravin' Crow Publishing (adult). She's the author of: *How to Write a Book: Park It, Get to Work* and its sequel, *Transplanted Heads: Your Muse Can't Write Worth Sh*t* (non-fiction); *Death in l'Acadie: a Kesk8a story*, *Refuge in l'Acadie: a Kesk8a story*, and *Trapped in l'Acadie: a Kesk8a story* (the first three of the planned six-book historical fiction series of which this is the fourth); *Graven Images* (fiction); *Vivie Goes to Hell in a Hatchback* (YA); *Mostly of Love & the Perils Thereof: The Sequel* and *The Closet Hides a Set of Stairs* (poetry). Under her pseudonym Christina Crowe, she has published *A Girl Dog's Breakfast*, scary stories and rude poems and *The Unkindest Cut: Short Creepy Movie Scripts*. Sherrill is also a screenwriter.

On her paternal grandmother's side, she is an Acadian descendant of Claude Guidry and Marguerite Petitpas.

Characters

Agada—Keskoua's friend and the mother of Sofia; a healer
Augustin—one of Marguerite's sons (real person)
Benny—Colonel Benjamin Church (real person, leader of the New England Rangers)
Bernie—young boy in Agada's village
Bobby—Young Bobcat Man; friend of Keskoua; "spy" (or is he?) for Louisbourg
Claude Guédry/Guidry—deceased; friend of Keskoua; husband of Marguerite Petitpas (the author's 7th great-grandfather) (real person)
Damnation—Nation, man who captured Keskoua in *Trapped*
Danny—young boy in Agada's village
Edward Gooden—previous surgeon at the fort, now living in Boston as Edward Gooden; a spy
Élisabeth—formal name of Eliza-Lester
Elisa-Lester—young woman studying to be a lawyer; friend of Bobby; "spy" (or is s/he?) for Louisbourg
Flower Stalk—Chief of the village next to where Agada lives; friend of Keskoua
François—brother-in-law of J-B; cousin of Paul; "taken" at 11 years of age (real person)
Franny—(Françoise), daughter of Marguerite (real person)

Geneviève—friend and teacher of Keskoua

Georges—Chef Georges at Mak and Keskoua's Mirligueche inn

Gi´gwesu—(Gig), Keskoua's brother

Guillaume—spy and pigeon messenger caretaker at Agada's village

Hammy, Abraham—former New England soldier/guard, friend of Agada; friend of Mak and Keskoua; pigeon messenger caretaker

Ian—the Scotsman; lover of Agada

James Mius—brother-in-law of J-B; brother of young François (real person)

J-B—Jean-Baptiste Guédry/Guidry; son of Claude and Marguerite (the author's 6th great-granduncle) (real person)

Jeune Jean—son of J-B; (Jean-Baptiste le Jeune) (real person)

John Missel—one of the men who took over the sloop (real person)

Jumping Robin—chief in Agada's village; successor of Matuwes

Keskoua—sixty-one years old in 1726

Little Bat—one of J-B's Spirit Questers in *Trapped*; now known as Bart Little, husband of Gracie Little (Little Gracie)

Little Gracie—niece of Mak; now known as Gracie Little and the wife of Bart Little

Lobster—(Marsel) one of the men who took over the sloop (real person)

Madeleine Marguerite Moise, Morning Star—wife of J-B; mother of Paul; sister of James and Philippe (real person)

Mak—Keskoua's husband

Marguerite Petitpas/Guédry—wife of Claude; mother of J-B, Pierre, and Augustin (the author's 7th great-grandmother) (real person)

Maggie Deux—Marguerite Brasseau; wife of Pierre Guidry dit LaBine (6th great grandmother of author) (real person)

Matuwes—former chief of the village next to Flower Stalk's village; friend of Keskoua

Paul—son of J-B; grandson of Marguerite; "taken" at 8 years of age (real person)

Philippe Mius—brother-in-law of J-B; brother of young François (real person)

Pierre Guidry dit LaBine—son of Marguerite; husband of Marguerite Brasseau, "Maggie Deux" (6th great grandfather of author) (real person)

Rich/Richard—Captain Rich as a former pirate; Captain Richard as a regular captain but "prefers just plain Captain"

Roxane/Roxie—young girl in Agada's village

Second Son, Secky—deceased husband of Agada; father of Sofia

Sofia—daughter of Agada and Secky (Second Son)

Solange—chef at Mak and Keskoua's Annapolis Royal inn; sister of Agada; friend of Keskoua

Su´n (Cranberry)—daughter of Keskoua; healer

Rabbit Woman—a resident of Keskoua's village, helped Keskoua when needed as a healer

Sachimus—crew member on the *Tryal* (real person)

Salmon—one of the men who took over the sloop; father of Young Dove Man (Lewis) (real person)

Samuel Doty—Captain Doty of the sloop, the *Tryal*; friend of Marguerite (real person)

Tugweit—healer in Mirligueche

Young Dove Man—Lewis, son of Salmon (real person)

Zeke—man who captured Keskoua in *Trapped*, now a friend of Mak and Keskoua

Vocabulary

amaljugwej: raccoon

apalqaqamej: chipmunk

apigjilu: skunk, Apigjilu na maqtaweg aq wape'g. *A skunk is black and white.*; Alternate forms: apigjilu'g, *skunks* (plural); apigjilu'l, *a skunk* (fourth person); Variant spelling(s): apugjilu (Nova Scotia)

apistanewj: marten, Apistanewj mawglu'lg ugtanguowe'im. *The marten's fur (hide) is very good*; apistanewjig, *martens* (plural); apistanewjl, *a marten* (fourth person)

aplíkmuj: rabbit, hare apli´gmujg, rabbits (plural); apli´gmujl, a rabbit (fourth person)

apo´qatej: woodpecker; variant spelling(s): apo´qajej (Nova Scotia), apo´qwatej Alternate forms: apo´qatejg, woodpeckers (plural); apo´qatejl, a woodpecker (fourth person)

app: repeat [please]; what did you say?

apugji´j: mouse; apigji´jg, mice (plural); apigji´jl, apigji´tl, a mouse (fourth person); Nutat apigji´j?; Do you hear the mouse?; Variant spelling(s): apugji´j (Nova Scotia)

apugsign, lynx

Apuknajit, February, Snow blinding month

atsco, as chu, or wad chu: hill

atu´tuejl, a squirrel (fourth person); atu´tuejg, squirrels (plural)

chenoo: a wendigo

e´e: yes

elue´wiet: crazy

emtesgit: arrogant, snooty

gajuewj: cat

gapjagwej: robin; gapjagwejg: robins; gapjagwejl: a robin

ga´qaquj: crow

gesalul, *I love you* (first person singular animate subject, second person singular animate object)

gesgamugwa´latl, gesgamugwa´toq: make vanish, make disappear, dissolve

gesmi´sit: speak in odd or unusual way; speak with a heavy accent

gesm´pisit: strange clothes

gesnugwai, *I am sick* (first person singular animate); gesnugwaieg, *We are sick* (first person dual exclusive animate); gesnugutieg, *We are sick* (first person plural exclusive animate)

gi´gwesu: muskrat

gi´gassuinu: teaser, joker

Giju´: Mother, Mom

gisigui´sgw: old woman, elderly woman. Ula gisigui´sgw teluisit Mali. This elderly woman's name is Mary. Alternate forms: gisigui´sgwaq, old women (plural); gisigui´sgul, an old woman (fourth person)

giwnig: otter; giwnigaq, otters (plural); giwnigal, an otter (fourth person) Giwnig na wisawamugsit wi´sisji´j. The otter is a small brownish animal.

glmuej: mosquito; glmuejg, mosquitoes (plural); glmuejl, a mosquito (fourth person)

gmu´jminn, a raspberry (fourth person); gmu´jming, raspberries (plural)

go´gwejij: spider (also means cancer). Go´gwejijg na mesgilgig aq apje´ji´jijig. Spiders are big and small. Variant spelling(s): awo´wejit (Bear River), awo´kejit (Unama´ki). Alternate forms: go´gwejijg, spiders (plural); go´gwejijl, a spider (fourth person); translation: Cancer. Meanings: cancer. Go´gwejij amujpa matnut. Cancer must be fought. Alternate forms: go´gwejijl, a cancer (fourth person)

go´gwejijua´pi: spiderweb. Go´gwejijua´pi maw weliangamgug ta´n tujiw na´gu´set saputasej. A spider web is pretty when the sun is shining through it. Variant spelling(s): awo´wejituo´pi (Bear River). Alternate forms: go´gwejijua´pi´l, spider webs (plural)

gtigiewinuj: drunkard; gtigiewinujg, drunkards (plural); gtigiewinujl, a drunkard (fourth person)

guow: pine; "Mesgilg guow gaqamit nignaq, A large pine stands in our yard." Alternate forms: guaq, pines (plural): guowl, a pine (fourth person)

gwitn: canoe; gwitnn, canoes

Haudenosaunee: a Nation ("Iroquois")

jenteg: quiet

kaksk´us, kaksk´ug: cedar(s)

kønsorganer, Danish: genitals

lentug: deer

Lnu Saqamaw: Chief

lutmaqan: gossip, rumor, hearsay

mala´sit: not doing well (health), progressing slowly

masgwi: white birch tree; masgwi´g, white birch trees (plural); masgwi´l, a white birch tree (fourth person)

massa: great

massawachusett: great mountain place

melgwisgat: nightmare; frightened (from nightmare); Miawitpa´qap ngwis melgwisgat aq mu´gisiapajinpagup. It was midnight when my son had a nightmare and then he couldn´t go back to sleep. Alternate forms: melgwisgai, I have a nightmare (first person singular animate); melgwisgaieg, We have a nightmare (first person dual exclusive animate); melgwisga´tieg, We have a nightmare (first person plural exclusive animate)

mesgei´: I am sorry

mess or mass: great

messatossec: Great hills mouth

Mi´kmaw, Mi´kmaq: Eastern Nation of Aboriginal People

mi´jan: excrement

mi´watm: I am grateful; mi´watmeg: we are grateful

moqopa´q: wine

mor: mother, mama, mom, in Danish

mpenzi: partner, wife/husband, etc., in Swahili

mtesgm: snake; mtesgmug, snakes (plural); mtesgml, a snake (fourth person)

mui´n: bear

mulumgwej groundhog, woodchuck; mulumgwejg, plural

munti: bag, sack

nalagit: energetic, swift, eager

natawinpiteget: good healer

na to´q: all right, OK

nepat: sleep, asleep

paqtesmul, a wolf (fourth person); paqtesmug, wolves (plural)

sec, sac or saco: mouth

snawe´l, snawe´g: sugar tree(s), maple(s)

so´qomu´jl, a minnow (fourth person); so´qomu´jg, minnows (plural). So´qomu´j na wesgowa´sit qospemg. The minnow lives in the lake.

sqolj: frog; Siggw na gaqatepiet sqolj nutut. In the spring one hears many a frog. (Variant spelling(s): atagali (NS).) Alternate forms: sqoljig, frogs (plural); sqoljl, a frog (fourth person)

su´n: cranberry

Tata´t: Father, Dad. Tata´t! Ge´ nipugtug la´tinej. Dad! let´s go to the woods.

tities: bluejay; titiesg: bluejays (plural); titiesl: a bluejay (fourth person) tmgwalignej; crane, heron; tmgwatinejg, cranes (plural); tmgwatinejl, a crane (fourth person), Enm´papga´timg jijuaqa nemu´t tmgwatignej etliwsget gigjiw sitmug, Going down the coast sometimes one can see a heron fishing for food by the shore.

toqosingig: sleep together

toqwa´q: autumn

tqoqwej: lynx, bobcat, wild cat. U´nama´gig apugsign telui´tasit tqoqwej. *In Cape Breton the bobcat (apugsign) is called a bobcat (tqoqwej).* Alternate forms: tqoqwejg, *wild cats* (plural); tqoqwejl, *a wild cat* (fourth person)

tugwiet: wake up, awaken

tutji´j: little daughter (Jugu´wa tutji´j apoqonmatinej. *Come little daughter, let us help each other.*

wasueg: flower, blossom, bloom, [blossoming flower]

Wendat: a Nation ("Huron")

wela´lin: thank you (wela´lin, na ta´n teliula´lin. Thank you, I do well by you.)

welaliog: thank you all

Appendix

Links

http://freepages.rootsweb.com/~guedrylabinefamily/genealogy/actofpiracypt1.html

http://freepages.rootsweb.com/~guedrylabinefamily/genealogy/actofpiracypt2.html

https://earlycanadianhistory.ca/2015/12/07/pirates-1726-the-regionalism-of-danger-in-the-early-northeast/

https://www.colonialsociety.org/node/1397

http://www.native-languages.org/mikmaq.htm

https://ap.gilderlehrman.org/essay/indian-slavery-americas#:~:text=Both%20before%20and%20during%20African,slaves%20and%20European%20indentured%20servants.

https://en.wikipedia.org/wiki/Treatment_of_the_enslaved_in_the_United_States

www.ingramcontent.com/pod-product-compliance
Lightning Source LLC
LaVergne TN
LVHW010059110826
845155LV00028B/409